Two Point Five Cheers
For The Library

Outi Pickering was born in Tampere, Finland, in 1952. She studied English and Italian at Turku University and later obtained a qualification in Library and Information Science. She worked in adult education and as a freelance translator before moving to the UK.

Outi now works as Assistant Librarian in the staff library of an NHS hospital, a job that has provided her with many of the ideas used in *Two Point Five Cheers for the Library*. She is married and has one daughter.

Outi Pickering

Two Point Five Cheers
For The Library

Olympia Publishers
London

www.olympiapublishers.com
OLYMPIA PAPERBACK EDITION

A CIP catalogue record for this title is
available from the British Library.

ISBN: 978-1-84897-614-6

(Olympia Publishers is part of Ashwell Publishing Ltd)

This is a work of fiction.
Names, characters, and places originate from the writer's imagination.
Any resemblance to actual persons, living or dead,
is purely coincidental.

First published *in 2015*

Olympia Publishers
60 Cannon Street
London
EC4N 6NP

Printed in Great Britain

To all my friends who have watched the Healthscare Library come to life.

ONE

EXCUSE ME, WHERE IS THE LIBRARY?

"This is what you get when the manager is away on jury service!" wailed Lucy Libris.

"This is what you get when you work for this Trust!" sobbed Mimosa MacAroon.

"This is what you get when you work for the NHS!" snarled Vladimir Logoff.

They were all huddling together in the hospital cleaning cupboard, the new location for Cardigan Bay Healthscare Library.

"Quiet, or you'll all do twenty minutes of shelf tidying!" thundered Simon Pendrive. He was still the library manager, even in the cleaning cupboard.

"What shelves?" Vladimir asked in that injured tone that he was so good at.

It was true. The empty shelves were all arranged along the shady corridor in a dangerous looking line, with the library's book and journal stock in crates piled up in front of the shelves.

***

It all started just before opening time that morning.

Mimosa MacAroon, Assistant Librarian, got out of her tiny white car near the main entrance to the hospital where the Healthscare Library was located. Incredibly lucky, she thought; usually there was nowhere to park by this time. She considered checking whether there was any post to pick up from Reception, but decided not to bother since Lucy would have done it already. Not because it was specifically the library assistant's job – any one of the team was supposed to pick up the post on the way upstairs, rather like in the olden days in the country when you brought in a bucket of water or an armful of firewood every time you came in. No, it was simply that Lucy was so very efficient. Mimosa couldn't imagine how the library would survive without Lucy; it was bad enough that she had to take holidays. Every time that happened, Simon swore that he would never allow her to go on leave again, but since the library manager had to stick to the rules, Lucy continued to take her annual leave as conscientiously as she did everything else. In fact, thought Mimosa, Lucy was perfect; that was her only fault.

At the end of the main corridor, Mimosa climbed the stairs and turned into the library corridor on the first floor. The door leading to it was propped open with a fire extinguisher. Mimosa frowned. Strictly forbidden! Who had done that? She heaved the fire extinguisher back on to its bracket. Then she looked at her watch: only twelve minutes to nine. Something was not right. Walking past the offices along the corridor, she pulled the key out of her handbag and was about to unlock the library door, when it opened and a brawny man in overalls brushed past her. He was carrying two crates of books piled precariously on top of each other.

"Hey, what's going on?" Mimosa asked in alarm. "Where are you taking those books?"

"Sorry, my love – we're from St. Ain Removals. The library is moving today." The man vanished into the corridor with his load.

Mimosa was speechless. The library manager had been on jury service the day before to help judge who would be the next Miss Trust, but why had he not informed them before that? Maybe the others had heard something that she, Mimosa, didn't know. She stepped in, and there was Vladimir coming to meet her.

"I only just got here, and there were these guys emptying the shelves and unplugging the computers. What's going on?" he asked crossly.

Lucy, the perfect library assistant, joined the others. She was slightly out of breath because she had nearly been knocked over by a removal man who couldn't see for the load he was carrying. It seemed that no one knew why their library was being emptied without warning. They only knew that Simon hadn't informed them of any impending moves – all he had told them was that the library would be moved in six months' time at the earliest – and Lucy remembered that Simon had said he might be late coming in this morning.

While the library staff were hastily comparing their non-existent notes, three more men with full crates marched out. Vlad considered tripping one of them and carrying the books back, but decided against it as a futile act of revenge. Mimosa dialled the number of Mr Moore-Gubbins, the Estates manager (she had to shoo away a removal man who was about to unplug the phone) and explained the situation to him.

"Ah, but I did email Simon several times. Funny thing he never got back to me, though. Simon Spindrift, isn't it?"

***

Simon Pendrive (stress on the second syllable) jumped off his trusty old bicycle at the main entrance to the hospital. He was in a good mood. The Miss Trust contest had been very enjoyable, and he was pleased that he had been invited to sit on the jury. It proved that the Library Services was an important department and the library manager a well-known person within the Trust. He had had enough of people forgetting about the library in their plans and reports, often not even knowing there was one.

In the main corridor he saw Simon Spindrift, a Very Senior Nurse.

"Hello, Simon," the nurse said, "can you imagine: my computer had been out of action for a fortnight, and when they finally fixed it, my inbox was full of messages from the Estates manager – something to do with the library move. He must have mixed up our names."

"How strange!" said Simon Pendrive. "I'd better give him a ring. Can't think why it should suddenly be so urgent; they've told us expressly that we won't move for at least another six months."

"Perhaps they're planning ahead for once," the other Simon suggested with a grin. He had had years of experience of dealing with the Powers That Be.

Simon continued briskly to the end of the main corridor, glancing as always at the portraits of managers and consultants that lined the walls, and – as always – wondered briefly and wistfully whether his portrait would hang there one day. He opened the door that led to the staircase, but was stopped by a medical student.

"Excuse me, but can you tell me where the library is?" the student asked him, looking rather flustered.

"Follow me," said Simon. "This way!"

"But..."

"I'm the library manager. Just follow me. It's not quite opening time yet, but I'll let you in," he added magnanimously. They trotted upstairs and turned the corner into the corridor, which led to the library. They could see immediately that the door was wide open. "That's what I mean," the student said. "It's not there."

Simon's heart seemed to stop beating. His library!

His library!

He ran the length of the corridor and into the empty entrance lobby. On the floor lay a hastily scribbled post-it note, which said THE LIBRARY HAS MOVED. In spite of the scribble, Simon recognised Mimosa's handwriting.

***

Simon looked at Vladimir, who had reminded his boss that no shelf tidying could be done when there were only empty shelves lining the Facilities corridor. Before he could think of a suitable reply, a small, elderly lady waddled up to them.

"So it is true, then! You've taken over my cleaning cupboard!" She turned accusingly to Vlad – perhaps because he was the tallest – who muttered something and waved in Simon's direction. The lady turned to address her complaint to Simon.

13

"Fancy turning up like that and never telling anybody! What have you done with my vacuum cleaner? I've been looking for it for hours. And as for cleaning fluids, don't you know that it's a Health and Safety issue, leaving them out like that?" She pointed to a bottle of bleach that had rolled between two crates. "I'll report you to my line manager!"

And she stomped off.

"I wish somebody *would* report us, and maybe we'd get out of this mess!" said Simon. He reached for his mobile phone, only to discover that there was no signal here in the depths of the hospital.

"What on earth does this mean?" a high-pitched voice demanded behind him. It was a tall lady whom Simon recognised instantly from the previous day's Miss Trust contest. She seemed to have materialised somehow from the shades of the corridor. "Don't you realise this is a Health and Safety issue? Any of these shelves could collapse on top of somebody – worst case scenario, on a patient or a visitor, in other words a tax payer. And if you'd done your fire awareness training, you would know better than to clutter a corridor with combustible materials. Besides, you ought to be ashamed of yourselves, invading the poor cleaner's space. I've overheard you lot in the staff canteen talking of accessing the tennis court – it's delusions of grandeur, that's what it is! Next thing you'll take over the hydrotherapy pool!"

She stormed off before any of them could point out to her that Tennis Court was not part of the Rehabilitation Unit but the newsletter of the regional health libraries' network, or TENNIS (The Electronic Nearly National Information System).

Simon leaned on a shelf unit. It swayed precariously, and he straightened himself again. He felt like crying. He couldn't remember crying since he was three years old and his father took away a copy of *Ben-Hur* from him when he'd been taken on a visit to Daddy's library and had pulled the book off the shelf. Little Simon had been upset. His father had looked very angry, but Simon hadn't known why. It had something to do with Simon turning the pages and having got as far as page ninety-seven. What was wrong with that? He had only wanted to see which page the library ownership stamp was on. The book couldn't be a bad one since it was called *Ben-Hur*, and Ben was the name of Simon's pet rabbit. Simon had made a decision there and then that he would be a librarian when he grew up – then he could look at any books he wanted to.

Simon roused himself. A fat lot of good it had done him, following his decision to be a librarian. He almost wished he had still been the little boy whose father was in charge of everything, libraries included.

"Can you imagine?" he said with a tired voice. "I voted for her!"

"Voted? Is she standing for the Council?" Vlad wondered. "Who is she, anyway?"

"Not the Council elections – the Miss Trust contest. She is Claire Twinsett, our new CHOKE."

The others looked blank, so Simon explained. "It's this new job you're supposed to have in all NHS Trusts now. It stands for CHief Officer for Knowledge and... actually, I'm not sure what the E is for. Experience? Electronics? Et cetera? Something like that, anyway. I've heard rumours she may become my next line manager."

At that moment, the Estates manager turned up.

"Oh, here you are! I've been looking for you everywhere! I'm so sorry about all this. Let me explain..." Mr Moore-Gubbins started, full of anxious benevolence.

Simon's eyes flashed suddenly. He came from a long line of distinguished librarians, and it was time he defended his library.

"You can explain later," he said with dignity. "Just ring St. Ain Removals now and tell them to come back on the double. I expect"—he took in his sorry team with a victorious glance—"*we* expect the library to be back in its original place by the end of the day. In the meantime, we'll go and have a coffee in the canteen. We deserve it."

TWO

THE TEMP FROM...

Vladimir Logoff, IT Librarian, whose work on attachments is second to none, was sitting at his desk a few days after the Healthscare Library had been restored to its original location. He was pondering on the fact that the Library Services had something called an SLA with various organisations, but now the letters SLA had come up as a new library code on the regional library management system.

How could people not get lost in this ever proliferating jungle of abbreviations, acronyms and initialisms? Vladimir had had to accept the fact that some of the junior doctors or JDRs who frequented the library were no longer known as SHOs but F1s, F2s (or was it FYs?) and who knows what, all different from the abbreviations he had learnt when he first started working for the NHS. He had always thought that F1 stood for Formula 1. Why did it suddenly also stand for Foundation 1? And how long were these particular abbreviations and acronyms going to be valid, anyway? There must be somebody lurking in the corridors of power who was only biding his (or her) time to make another change, judiciously timed to bring honour and advancement to its inventor.

Forget about SLAs, F1s, corridors of power, and Powers That Be! He, Vladimir Logoff, would one day be known as the founder of the MANHATTAN, or MANagerial HATred of TANgentialities, movement. After that, he could rightly be called KING – which could be deciphered as Knowledge and INformation Governor – both within their Trust and the TENNIS network, perhaps even nationally! He knew that Lucy had long been hankering after an ASBO (or that's what she called the Advanced System of Book Ordering), so she would be sure to support him in his fight against red tape. In fact Lucy had recently tried to order the ASBO software for the library, but the Trust's electronic procurement system had chewed and garbled her requisition so that the software package had been delivered to the nearby police station. Simon wouldn't object to the new movement either, since he was always complaining about the Never-Ending Expenditure of Time.

Vlad swung round on his chair and was about to go and find Lucy. Now was the time to launch the MANHATTAN movement, and Lucy would have the honour of being the first person to hear about it. But at that moment the library manager came in.

"Listen Vlad," Simon began, with a worried look on his face. "I'm afraid Lucy has just rung to say she has been sent on a long term sick, due to COCHRANE."

"Due to *what*??" Vlad asked, puzzled.

"Oh Vlad, surely you know what COCHRANE stands for? COffee and CHocolate Related Aggressive NErvousness. Now, I want you to take the F1 library induction on Thursday in Lucy's absence. The contact person is called Mika Häkkinen. I'll spell that for you..."

And so it happened that the launch of the MANHATTAN movement was put on the back burner because the Healthscare Library was short staffed due to the library assistant being on long term sick leave. The unexpected move into the cleaning cupboard had been too much for her delicate nerves.

Simon had of course phoned NHS Professionals immediately to ask for a temporary worker, but they hadn't been able to provide one. All they could do was to recommend another agency. To Simon's relief, TempLate promised to send one of their employees the following working day, and – even better – said that Harry would be available for several weeks if necessary.

Harry Hoakes arrived thus on Monday, and Mimosa duly introduced him to the workings of the library. She had an induction checklist, which was just as well since they were interrupted several times by phone calls meant for the hospital kitchen. It was unfortunate that the number for the kitchen was so similar to the library number; they had quite enough to do in any circumstances, let alone now that they were short staffed and trying to bring a temp up to speed.

Harry seemed a cheerful yet calm sort of person, a promising combination of characteristics. The only thing that aroused Mimosa's suspicion was Harry's eagerness to convince her that he loved books. "They're my best friends," he told her. Mimosa knew from experience that some people loved books only too well, sometimes taking them out for walks.

Mimosa did an hour's work with Harry on fire and security procedures, locations of useful items, and everyday routines such as handling cash. More delicate matters such as handling customers would be best approached after a coffee break. She therefore went into the staff room to put the kettle on and left Harry in the office, where he had been settled behind Lucy's desk. Through the open door she heard two customers ask whether they could use the photocopier. "Oh dear, that's a good question," was Harry's answer.

Mimosa bit her lip. Hadn't she had explained to him about the photocopier? She abandoned the kettle and returned to the office.

Thankfully, the rest of Monday was fairly uneventful, except that Harry annoyed Vladimir by offering to help with a tricky IT problem. "I've almost completed the first module of the Computer Driving Licence," the temp announced proudly.

On Tuesday, Harry was reprimanded by the cashier for putting down "Ann Visitor" in the cash receipt book. His excuse was that it was boring to write "student" or "visitor" every time you didn't know the name of the customer who made a payment. He also evoked the wrath of the Chief Executive Officer by opening two of his letters, which had been accidentally delivered to the library. It was all Mimosa's fault of course: if she hadn't told Harry to put in a compliment slip explaining what had happened, the CEO would have been none the wiser when he eventually received the letters. Or perhaps it was the fault of the Post Room staff for having delivered the letters to the wrong department in the first place. At least that was Harry's opinion.

On Wednesday, Harry would have upset Lucy if she had been there, when he leafed through her diary in order to find whether there was a Friday the 13th in the year. Mimosa fairly snatched the diary from him and locked it in her own desk.

Harry also annoyed Mimosa when he answered the phone and was asked a question regarding interlibrary loans. "Just a moment, I'll transfer you," he said cheerfully and then continued in a different voice: "Plim, plom! Interlibrary loans, how can I help you?" Mimosa decided it was best in this case *not* to snatch the receiver from his hand.

On Thursday, Harry scandalised several TENNIS libraries by adding a couple of repetitive syllables to a book title on stuttering. Of course it was Mimosa's fault for having allowed Harry to try out his skill in cataloguing on the regional system, or at least that was the opinion of the other librarians. He also infuriated the Estates when he propped the reading room window open with a heavy duty stapler, which then fell down and narrowly missed Mr Moore-Gubbins, who happened to be passing. "I'll fill in an incident report, and then you'll be sorry!" he shouted up to the open window, but Mimosa was the only one who heard the threat, and she thought it was best ignored.

On Friday, Harry finally angered the library manager. This is how it happened:

A library user came in and enquired about a book that he couldn't find on the shelf. Harry – who admittedly had learnt to use the catalogue very quickly – checked the details. Mimosa was busy at her desk, but keeping an ear open in Harry's direction all the time.

"It's overdue. Long overdue, in fact. Oh dear, it's Dr Achinside again: I noticed this morning she's had overdues before," Harry laughed.

Mimosa froze in disbelief. How could Harry behave like that? Hadn't he grasped the first thing about confidentiality? What should she do now – should she tell him to shut up immediately? If she did, then the reader's attention would be drawn to Harry's unprofessional behaviour. But if she didn't, then what else might the man disclose?

The reader left before Mimosa could make up her mind. She was about to speak to Harry, but was summoned to Simon's office across the lobby. He was wearing his Expression 3B, which he had never before directed at Mimosa.

"I heard every word. Haven't you taught that man about confidentiality?" Simon asked Mimosa icily. "What *did* you teach him in your induction?"

Mimosa felt near to very unprofessional tears. It was unfair to put the blame on her, but how could she make Simon understand that? Wasn't it obvious to him by now that their temp simply didn't operate along the same lines as other people?

She drew a deep breath and looked Simon in the eye. "I followed the induction checklist to the letter, and it's not my fault if he behaves like that," she said as firmly and calmly as she could. This seemed to reassure Simon a little, and his facial expression relaxed by one stage to Expression 3A.

"Very well then, go and talk to him again. I'll take this phone call," he said and reached for the phone that was ringing.

In a minute, the trembling Mimosa was called back into the library manager's office.

"Lucy has just rung in to say she's been given another week of sick leave. I'm afraid NHS Professionals still can't give us a temp, and we can't have another one from TempLate," Simon explained with despair in his voice. Before Mimosa had time to respond to this dire news, they heard how the phone rang in the other office, and they heard how Harry took the call.

"Kitchen?" he said. "No, this is the library. This is where we cook the books."

Simon didn't wait to hear the end of the conversation. He consulted the list of TENNIS libraries quickly and then dialled a number.

"Hello, is that Joint Orthopaedic? This is Simon from the library at Cardigan Bay. We have an interlibrary loan request, and you're the only library that holds the title... Yes, our library code is CARB... It's called *Dealing with the Employee from Hell*. Can you make it first class, please, and mark it to the library manager's attention? It's very urgent."

THREE

HOW MOBILE WAS MY TROLLEY

Cardigan Bay Healthscare Library had cause for celebration: Lucy had at last returned from her sick leave. She had been strictly warned against any excess of caffeine and chocolate, or she might succumb to another attack of COffee and CHocolate Related Aggressive NErvousness. So, there she was, sipping her camomile tea while her colleagues were downing the morning's second and third cups of coffee in the back office, which they called the staff room.

Mimosa was tidying the coffee table from its usual covering of sundry journals and magazines. "Can I throw away this Health Libraries' magazine? It's six months old." She waved a copy of *HEL's Bells* in her colleagues' direction.

"No, let me have a look," Lucy said. She was fingering her bun nervously, or so it seemed to Simon. Was Lucy fully recovered, or had she returned to work too early? Simon cast a long look at her. But before he had time to decide whether she really looked well enough, Lucy burst out in indignation, making Simon jump in his seat.

"Look at all these libraries that have had a facelift! And there are some completely new libraries as well. Where does all the money come from, and why don't we have any of it?"

She squeezed her bun in her hand, causing it to disintegrate into crumbs.

They all bent over the magazine. The pictures did look pretty impressive. One library had a highly polished, shiny floor, but Vlad was quick to point out it must be a Health and Safety hazard. Another one was very large and even more impressive.

"Look at that! Wow! Who could have afforded that?" Mimosa gasped with delight. "That's the Library of Congress in Washington," Vlad said drily. "No NHS money wasted there."

"Here's a library that has a noodle bar upstairs," Lucy said jealously. "Why can't we do anything to improve our profile, Simon?" She should have known the answer: there was no money. Secretly, Simon would have liked to add that there was little hope of any refurbishment if the library was to be relocated within the next six months, but he dared not mention the possibility of a move in case Lucy got upset.

It was as if they had suddenly noticed their surroundings for the first time. They all stared sadly at the walls of the staffroom, pock-marked with attempts to remove old Blu-Tack with which posters and notices had been stuck down. The other rooms didn't look much better; the walls and doors bore signs of scuffing by feet, trolleys, vacuum cleaners – not that they came along very often – and more Blu-Tack marks here and there. The carpets had unsightly marks of spilled coffee and tea, where readers had brought in their drinks against regulations or library staff had hurried to answer the phone while carrying a mug. Adonis the cleaner was furious every time a new spot appeared in the carpet. "It's like a leopard," he grumbled. "Only not so pretty."

They were becoming more and more depressed because so many lucky, shining, elegant libraries existed somewhere out there, and theirs wasn't one of them. Simon was about to declare that it was time to go and do some work, when a library user put his head in with a wide smile on his face.

"Can I disturb you all for a minute?" he asked. "You've helped our team so much with our research that we thought I should come and say thank you. You carried out a literature search for us, provided the interlibrary loans in record time, and even helped us to interpret some of the foreign language articles. We've written our report for the *Lancet* now and have acknowledged your help. It will probably be published in a few months. In the meantime, here is a gift voucher for the garden centre – we thought you might like to buy some flowers or potted plants to cheer the place up a bit."

They looked at each other in amazement, and then at the reader; finally Simon remembered his manners and thanked the research team for their generosity.

When the visitor had gone, Simon turned to his colleagues.

"Well done, team!" he said. "I'll do the washing up if Mimosa looks after the library – Vlad, you and Lucy can go to the garden centre in your car."

Life was good, Simon thought as he piled up the mugs in the washing up bowl. The team was together again, a mention in the *Lancet* had been promised, and a little contribution was being made to brighten up their surroundings. And then of course there was the handsome display unit, which they had ordered for new books. It was to be put in the reading room, and Simon was very much looking forward to it – and so was Mimosa as their acquisitions librarian.

It arrived the same afternoon, arousing a few questions because the NHS Cargo van driver had announced he had a mobile trolley to deliver. No one was quite sure what a mobile trolley was, as a trolley was supposed to be mobile by definition. If on the other hand it was a trolley intended for mobiles, who on earth would have enough mobile phones to need a trolley to hold them, except possibly a mobile phone shop? But the delivery note clearly specified the hospital library, not a mobile phone shop. The problem was that none of the team had any knowledge of ordering a trolley. The driver therefore retired into the café to wait for the outcome of the discussion.

After consulting their paperwork as well as the online version of NHS Cargo's ordering system, the library team came to the conclusion that this must be the new display unit they had been waiting for. Lucy – who had barely returned from the trip to the gardening centre – was sent downstairs to fetch the driver from the café. To her dismay, the man told her he had not been tasked with carrying the consignment anywhere. All he was willing to do was to dump the boxes at Reception, and the receptionist on duty wouldn't hear of it because their area was already quite congested.

Lucy's pleading eyes were rapidly filling with tears. The van driver, no doubt wanting to avoid a scene, grudgingly agreed to take the boxes upstairs. Unfortunately he had forgotten to bring a trolley with him – the kind that porters used for carting loads around – but a passing porter was willing to lend his trolley for half an hour. Lucy reassured the driver that there was a lift at the end of the main corridor, as they proceeded in a slow march-past under the eyes of the managers' and consultants' portraits that adorned the walls.

The driver struggled to balance his uneven load, and Lucy suffered agonies because she was so sorry for him and wondered if she should have tried to help. She knew there would be another long corridor ahead as they stepped out of the lift.

Of course it was out of the question to ask the driver to assemble the unit, so he left them with sundry large and heavy boxes of shelves, uprights, back panels, and whatever else. Lucy therefore put in a call to the Estates to get a carpenter to put the unit together. Mimosa was annoyed that a man should be called to do the job, but Simon pointed out that she and Lucy simply weren't strong enough. He himself would have liked to have a go at it, but assembling furniture wasn't his forte, and besides, a library manager had a lot of other responsibilities. As for Vladimir, it was just as well that he was in the IT suite delivering a training session; he had a tendency to treat anything new as material for experimentation.

At that moment there was a phone call from the furniture company. They said too many shelves had been delivered, so they would send a driver to collect them that very afternoon. Mimosa pointed out that the driver wouldn't know what to pick up since no assembly instructions had been provided. The kind lady at the other end suggested the driver could assemble the trolley so that any leftover parts could then be taken away. Mimosa agreed, but doubted in her mind whether the second driver would be willing to assemble the trolley since the first driver had been so reluctant even to bring the parts upstairs.

She was right. Two men turned up, but when she told them what the plan was, the older one looked daggers at her.

After the offer of a cuppa (which was declined) they relented and said they would assemble the unit sufficiently to see what the parts were, rather than risk taking back the wrong ones and having to make another trip. They started to open the boxes and spread the contents on the floor of the lobby, causing library users to perform highly artistic patterns of steps over and around the materials when they wanted to access the reading room. One of the men cut his finger in the packaging so that Lucy had to run for the first aid kit. Her ministrations slightly soothed the man, and a further offer of coffee was accepted. After that, they progressed more rapidly and completed the job ten minutes before the library was due to close. That was when they discovered that the number of shelves was correct after all, so nothing was left over for them to take away.

"There we are, me dear," the older one said to Mimosa, beaming at her with pride. "Where d'you want it?" She held open the door of the reading room and pointed to the area where the display unit was intended to stand. The men each took a firm hold of the unit, and with a tremendous cry of "ee-op" they gave it a push. The trolley shuddered and wobbled perilously, and Mimosa let go of the door and withdrew to safety. The door swung shut, trapping the younger man's hand between it and the trolley. He emitted an unprintable word, and Mimosa apologised and opened the door again. This time the trolley was pushed through successfully and steered into its place, but with the sloping display shelves facing the wall.

The men were not very pleased when Mimosa pointed out that they ought to turn the trolley round, but she was adamant. "It's called a *mobile* book trolley," she said firmly.

"Therefore you can turn it." She decided against any further sarcastic comments, for there was Lucy with a sign saying NEW TITLES DISPLAY, which she had created in the meantime; there was Simon standing at the door and smiling approvingly, and there was Dr Terremoto coming in and looking impressed. Mimosa waited by the door as he approached. "We have a new piece of furniture," she told him. "You'll see in a minute – I've got a batch of new books to go on it."

"Very nice," he said, looking at her with his oh so brown eyes. "And flowering plants on the windowsill, I see. I must come here more often."

Yes, Mimosa thought. *I agree!*

FOUR

THE LAST BISCUIT

The CARB staff each had a clearly definable relationship with biscuits. Lucy rather liked them but often felt guilty when a colleague saw her nibbling a biscuit at her desk. Not that anyone ever commented, the problem was entirely in Lucy's mind. Vladimir on the other hand had no problems with biscuits, unless it was the fact that the library often ran out of them and there was no shop on site where they could top up their supply. Mimosa loved a few biscuits every now and then, with a cup of coffee of course, but she was worried she might put on weight. Simon was the only one who could contemplate a packet of biscuits with complete unconcern, but as library manager he might be expected to offer one to a visitor and was therefore keen to keep an eye on supplies. The last biscuit had often vanished a few minutes before an important visit.

"Just follow the crumb trail and you'll find the culprit," Mimosa advised Simon with a meaningful glance at Vladimir. But Simon said it was beneath him to start a new career as a biscuit detective.

It was naturally out of the question to charge biscuits to the library budget, so they all took turns bringing in a packet. This, however, was dependent on people's memory and often led to arguments between Mimosa and Vladimir because they accused each other of missing their turn. Simon therefore decreed that they would each put a certain amount of money into a kitty every week, and Lucy was tasked with buying the biscuits. But it was surprising how often his staff found they didn't have ready money when it came to contributing.

Finally, the exasperated manager announced that everyone was to bring in their own supplies, and he would see to it that there was always a packet in case of visitors. The others agreed it was worth giving the new system a try.

Mimosa for one was pleased. Now she could buy a box of her favourite biscuits and wouldn't have to worry about sharing them, especially as Vladimir seemed to prefer the same kind. Her only concern was that Vlad might raid the box if she left it on her desk. Would he dare? The box was too big to fit into any of her desk drawers. What should she do? Then she had an idea. Elementary, my dear Watson; why hadn't she thought of it before?

Lucy was relieved that there would be fewer arguments from now on – at least about biscuits. She bought a large packet of her favourite kind on the way to work the following morning. But where would she keep it? It was too big to fit into her desk drawers, however tidy she kept them, and the deep drawer was reserved for her handbag. At last she thought of a plan and smiled to herself.

Vlad was pleased, too. Now he wouldn't have to pretend to be polite and make sure that Ms MacAroon had had her share of biscuits. She seemed to like the same kind of biscuits as he did, just to be awkward. But where the hell could he keep his store? His desk drawers were already full of manuals and gadgets that he needed in his IT experiments. Ah, but there was an obvious place...

Simon sighed with relief. He was proud of himself for having solved this staff management problem; now he could have some peace and quiet in his library. But he couldn't really keep the visitors' biscuits in his office; the team would only tease him and claim that he really wanted them for himself, even though they knew full well that he was quite neutral with regard to biscuits. OK, he could eat one just to keep company, but that was all, he wasn't a connoisseur. He had chosen this variety because he had seen Lucy eat them, so it must be a suitable one for visitors.

So, where should he store the biscuits? In the crockery cupboard in the staff room? Of course, where else! But... his staff might not prove trustworthy here. He had intended to offer them a biscuit or two out of the visitors' packet one day, maybe when they had been especially busy and needed some managerial encouragement, but he did not intend to allow them a free hand. Hmm... He got up, took the biscuit packet and slipped quietly into the staff room.

For an hour or so, all was well. All was calm. A few readers returned their books to the library office, Simon had a phone call from another library manager, and the others carried on with their jobs as expected. For once, there seemed to be time to get on with those jobs.

Lucy had finished the library registrations which they had had as a result of the monthly Trust induction. Quite a few new starters, and most of them had wanted to join the library, so she had been busy entering their details into the membership database. Now she would send them their library cards. She noticed she had run out of envelopes and got up to go into the staff room, where the stationery was kept in a large tambour cupboard. While she was there, she could get a biccy or two out of her secret store. If anyone else was around, she would have to get only the envelopes, but the thought of those biscuits made her hope everyone else was busy with their own tasks.

As Lucy was about to step out of the office, she noticed Simon crossing the lobby. He must have come out of the staff room. He was carrying something, but Lucy couldn't quite see what it was. A packet of biscuits? She waited a few seconds, pretending she hadn't noticed him. Then she went into the staff room, trying to make her action look natural. The tambour cupboard was half open, but that in itself didn't signify anything. She pushed the folding door open completely and felt behind the box of long envelopes, which she had chosen because the space was larger than the space behind the full size envelope boxes. There was nothing there. Her heart began to beat faster. She felt again: nothing.

Tears filled Lucy's eyes. Her boss, whom she had always liked and trusted, had sneaked in and taken her biscuits. What made it even worse was the fact that he had always claimed not to care about biscuits. But how had he guessed Lucy's secret? She tried to calm down so that she could go back to her desk. She could not confront Simon with this, she simply couldn't. She would have to live with it, but her trust in Simon had gone for ever. She had enough presence of mind to pick up a bundle of envelopes before she pulled the cupboard door closed.

Mimosa had been asked to find some information for one of the occupational therapists. The clinical databases they all could access with their NHS user names provided a part of the information, but she knew there was a website that might give a different angle to the problem. She typed in the web address and clicked. A familiar message appeared at the top of the screen. Cookies... allowing cookies... The search vanished from her mind, and the image of a mug of coffee and a couple of her favourite biscuits replaced it. Her favourite biscuits, those delicious melt-in-the-mouth, chocolate-covered, caramel-filled biscuits, which she had a box of, and the box was in her safe hiding place!

She got up from her desk and walked into the staff room, hoping her action looked casual. She pushed back the door of the tambour cupboard, cursing under her breath because the rolling action made such a noise. If somebody came in, she would grab a couple of pens and say something meaningless and cheerful. She pushed her hand into the space behind the box which contained pens and felt along there. Nothing. Strange – she was sure she had hidden the biscuit box behind the pens. She had chosen the place because the box would fit there. She put her hand in again: nothing. She began to breathe faster. Could she have made a mistake and checked the wrong shelf? To make sure, she began to pull out boxes from the shelf below. Who was the thief? Vlad, of course! She should have chosen a shelf with something bigger than a box of pens. Envelopes for instance.

Mimosa was so frantic she didn't hear the footsteps on the worn carpet. She swung back only when she heard Vlad's voice.

"What are you looking for, Samosa?"

"How dare you call me Samosa? Isn't it bad enough you're a thief?" Mimosa's face was contorted with rage, and her ginger hair seemed to be aflame. The IT librarian might have admired the effect for half a second if he hadn't been so angry himself.

"That really takes the biscuit, Samosa. You can call me anything you like, but don't call me a thief, or I'll report you to Simon!"

"No need to report, this racket is loud enough to be heard at the other end of the library!" The library manager had appeared at the door, and his voice was as sharp as a whiplash. How long had they enjoyed peace and quiet this morning? An hour? Was that too much for those two?

Lucy rushed out of her office. What was the row about? Her biscuits? Oh, why had she ever thought of hiding them...? It was all her fault.

Mimosa had been working like a fury, and most of the contents of the shelf now lay on the floor. She ignored Simon and only stopped when she found a packet of biscuits. A packet, not a box. How –

"My biscuits!" Lucy let out a squeal and pushed Simon aside, snatching her packet like a long lost friend.

"Just a minute, Lucy," Simon said quickly, stepping up to the cupboard. "Those are the biscuits that I—" He hesitated. He suddenly felt embarrassed to admit that he, Simon Pendrive (stress on the second syllable), Library Services Manager, had hidden a packet of biscuits in the stationery cupboard so that his staff wouldn't find it.

From there, it was a fairly short step to unravelling the mystery. Mimosa and Vlad had chosen the same shelf for their biscuits, which were of the same variety, but hidden them a few inches apart; Simon and Lucy had done the same but using the shelf below. Mimosa had to admit that Vlad was not a thief, and by way of apology, she offered to share her box with him even though he had one of his own. Lucy was immensely relieved to find that her boss was not a thief although she didn't tell anyone of her suspicions. Simon for his part felt that he hadn't trusted his team as much as he should have done, so he offered to share the contents of the visitors' packet with them.

Thus peace was restored again and a large number of biscuits consumed. Lunchtime came, but Simon was the only one who still had an appetite for his sandwich. He couldn't understand how anyone could make such a fuss about biscuits. Let them eat cake!

FIVE

FOR WHOM THE BELL RINGS

Change is inevitable; sometimes it's for the better, sometimes for the worse. Some changes took place in the hospital, which had an effect on the Healthscare Library, and the library team spent endless coffee breaks discussing whether those changes belonged to the first category or the second.

For a long time, security doors were pretty rare in the hospital. People wandered in and out; patients, carers and visitors were expected to keep to their designated areas and not to cross the threshold of the staff library or other limited access areas. In other words, they were expected to obey rules. Over the years, however, human nature changed (*society* changed, as Mimosa repeatedly pointed out) and people began to explore their boundaries. In the hospital, this meant that people who were not employed by the Trust sometimes entered the library and had to be either welcomed or gently ushered out of the door, depending on their information needs and on their general behaviour. A more problematic but invisible category of visitor was thieves. This of course was not completely new, since all public buildings suffered from the same problem. Pickpockets slipped into offices while the occupant nipped down the corridor for two minutes; determined looking men in boiler suits called to remove a piece of office furniture or a brand new computer while the manager was away.

"Interesting," an American visiting researcher remarked to Mimosa, whose stolen purse had been found (minus its contents, of course) behind the cistern in the men's toilet. "That's exactly where pickpockets would hide a wallet on our university campus. I don't think it's an international league of criminals, so I guess it's down to human nature."

Finally, the Powers That Be decided that enough was enough. The corridor leading to the library was to have a new lock put on the door and a doorbell installed at that end; library staff would hear the bell, walk down the corridor, and open the door – or not, as they saw fit. The device was quite simple. Al Monte from Estates came one morning, drilled a small hole or two in the doorpost at the far end of the corridor and stuck the transmitter, a little white box, on. The corresponding box, which delivered the sound, was simply placed on the windowsill in the library lobby.

"You'll hear the bell all right," Al promised. "It says on the package that the bell has a radius of fifty yards."

Mimosa, Lucy and Vladimir spent an interesting couple of hours taking turns to ring the bell and to answer the door. The problem was that if the receiver was shifted ever so little, it was shadowed by a bit of the doorpost or the edge of a bookshelf and could not be heard in the library.

"Fifty yards my foot," Vladimir grunted. "Maybe on Salisbury plain. We can't stick a notice on the receiver saying DO NOT MOVE – it's not big enough for that. Your turn to go down the corridor, Samosa."

"Don't call me—" Mimosa began angrily, but a doctor who was sitting at a computer in the lobby interrupted her.

"I'm sorry, but I'm actually trying to work, and that doorbell is getting really irritating. What exactly are you trying to do?" he demanded to know.

"Fine tuning the doorbell so that your patients won't come into the library while you're working here," Vlad retorted. He marched down the corridor and pressed the soft rubber button so hard that it stuck in the down position, causing the bell to ring continuously. Lucy thought she could see half a smile on her colleague's lips when he returned, but that was surely just her imagination since Vlad never smiled. The enraged doctor jumped up and walked out, muttering something about libraries not being the quiet places they used to be. Vlad then followed him and unstuck the rubber button.

Finally the exact spot was determined where the sound of the bell was picked up successfully and relayed to the library. The receiver was fixed on this spot with Blu-Tack to avoid accidental shifting – Lucy's idea, of which she was very proud – and the readers had a bit of peace at last. Mimosa, Lucy and Vladimir returned to their desks, and Simon could stop peering out of his office to see how they were getting on with the new device. Fortunately they had been given keys to the corridor; it would have been typical to have a new lock installed without delivering the keys, Simon thought. It still rankled a little that he hadn't been consulted before the decision was made to install a doorbell leading to his library. In fact, they hadn't been informed about the bell at all until the same morning. But it probably meant that the library move would not take place for a good long time now. The mere thought of such a disruption made the library manager shudder.

Before the end of the day, several things had happened: (a) five extra sets of keys were delivered, never mind that Simon hadn't ordered any (b) eight current and two new library users, two patients, and one porter had all wanted to gain access to the library and had rung the bell (c) three of them had complained about the new system being put into place without advance notice (d) four people had wanted not the library, but the consultant whose office was in the corridor (e) Mimosa had twice refused to go and open the door because she claimed it was Vlad's turn (f) Simon had reprimanded her for being so uncooperative.

"I know what we should do, Simon," Lucy suggested. "Couldn't we make this into an evidence-based exercise? We'll note how many times we have to go down the corridor, and then maybe we can persuade the Powers That Be that the doorbell interferes with our work."

"Good thinking, Lucy," Simon said, visibly relieved. "We'll keep a doorbell log for three weeks. That should be long enough."

"But we get a lot of exercise this way," Vladimir pointed out. "It's beneficial."

"Then why didn't you go down when it was your turn?" Mimosa's anger flared again.

"Speak for yourself! It was you who refused—"

Simon's face slowly began to assume Expression 3B, so Vladimir slunk back into his office and Mimosa hastily piled some books on her desk, trying to hide behind them.

At the end of the second week, the doorbell stopped functioning. Aspiring visitors waved their arms frantically behind the glass door at the bottom of the corridor, hoping to attract attention. Some rang the library on their mobile phones; this produced a more consistent result. Al Monte was called in to investigate, and his diagnosis was that the battery of the transmitter had run out. Lucy was duly told to order a couple of batteries online from NHS Cargo. The order was returned because three dozen batteries was the minimum quantity and delivery time was two weeks unless there was a clinical need, so the frustrated library assistant bought a battery from the corner shop with her own money on her way home.

At the end of the three-week trial period, the library team had answered the doorbell one hundred and three times between them. Simon triumphantly wrote a memo – not forgetting to include the magic words Evidence Based Practice – and delivered it to the Powers That Be. This had an immediate effect: Al Monte turned up the following day and removed the doorbell.

"I wonder if there was a clinical need?" Lucy remarked, a picture of innocence. The others ignored the remark since Lucy was never known to display any signs of sarcasm, but Simon pointed out to her (just in case she had spoken out of naivety) that clinical needs affected ordering stationery items such as lever arch files, not unsolicited doorbell installations. Mimosa reflected on the remark afterwards and came to the conclusion that Lucy was after all only intermittently perfect.

A rumour started that an intercom would be installed at the far end of the corridor or possibly downstairs, but no one took such a rumour seriously. At any rate it wouldn't happen until they had all retired.

They proved to be wrong. One morning, the door at the bottom of the stairs was locked and resisted Simon's attempts to open it. Then Vladimir arrived and pointed out the security pad, which had sprung up overnight on the wall by the door. There were buttons above it with little labels saying LIBRARY and TOP FLOOR and INFECTION CONTROL. They pressed LIBRARY, but nothing happened. A few other people arrived, but they of course had no access, either.

"Try buzzing the library," one of them suggested. "There's always somebody there. They're really helpful."

Simon glowered at the man, but then realised he should have taken the remark as a compliment. After five minutes of pressing each button in turn, they gave up and phoned the library. It was their good luck that Mimosa and Lucy had already arrived, apparently only minutes before the door had been locked. Lucy ran downstairs to let everybody in, but it was obvious that this was going to be impossible; they couldn't come down every time somebody phoned and asked for access. Why was there no counterpart to the intercom upstairs? Most importantly – said Simon – why had they not been informed, but been suddenly locked out of their workplace? He was not at all amused when Vladimir suggested the logical conclusion was that they could all go home now.

Simon dialled the number of the Estates manager, only to discover that he was on annual leave. Vlad thought it best to put the kettle on. Just then Al Monte turned up with another man, and together they started drilling and banging at the doorpost of Mimosa and Lucy's office.

"It's here that you want the intercom, isn't it?" Al suddenly asked, turning to the ladies. "Not the other side of the door? Or in Simon's office?"

"It would help if you explained what it's all about," Mimosa replied acidly. Then she repented. The men were

43

only installing something the Powers That Be had told them to install.

"It's an intercom, only you've got the deluxe version here with a camera," Al said, looking important. "Somebody buzzes for the library downstairs, you pick up the receiver and ask them what it is they want, and you can see who it is. Then if you don't like the look of them, you slam the phone down." He followed this with a loud laugh. Then he explained that the security pad at the bottom of the stairs would eventually be activated so that people could let themselves in if they had a staff access badge. But that would take a long time, so they'd better get used to intercom calls in the meantime.

Incredible but true: the system worked. Simon went downstairs himself to test it, and soon the others heard a piercingly shrill sound from the mysterious machine. Mimosa picked up the receiver and saw on the little screen what looked like a slightly wobbly moonlit view of the area in front of the door downstairs, with a slice of the library manager's shoulder and what she took to be a wisp of hair.

"Who is it?" she asked with an air of importance.

"It's me, Simon. Let me in!" the voice came loud and clear.

But Mimosa still remembered how she had been told off for arguing with Vlad. "I can't see you very well," she replied. "Please step back so that I get a full view of your face." Simon stepped back obediently, and a slightly distorted image of a bluish head and shoulders floated into view.

"All right, I've identified you now," Mimosa continued. "But promise me a rise in salary first."

"I can't!" Simon snapped. "You know that very well. It's a question of your salary band, and that's not due for a rise. Let me in, I've got things to do!" It was clear even on the ghostly-looking screen that Expression 3B was beginning to take shape.

"I think we ought to formulate a policy about this intercom first," Mimosa went on calmly, ignoring the danger signs. "Can you wait while I consult the deputy librarian?" She turned away to call Vlad.

Lucy couldn't stand the mounting tension any longer. She pushed Mimosa aside and pressed the button, which released the locking mechanism downstairs. Simon must have heard the click and pushed the door open, because he vanished from view. That was when Mimosa remembered she had some urgent business in the stacks on the second floor.

"It was a good try," Vlad consoled her before she made a dash for the stacks. "By the way, who's going to let the first of us in tomorrow morning?"

SIX

THE WRITE STUFF

Mimosa was sitting in her office reading the latest *HEL's Bells*. She was feeling pleased with herself for keeping up with the *Bells* for once; there was a lot going on in health libraries nationwide. But her good humour vanished when she came across the phrase 'man-aged learning environment' on page nineteen.

Mimosa was furious. Yet another case of that wonderful creature, man, being used as an example! Why not woman? Why not person? Why not... She looked at the page again and turned crimson. Oops... what a good thing she hadn't exclaimed aloud. That little hyphen was there for a purpose. Why did words have to be split at the end of a line?

On the other side of the office, Lucy sighed as she opened the stationery consignment from NHS Cargo. It was a large blue plastic crate, so large that a small person like Lucy could barely handle it, but when she removed the lid, all she found was one box of twelve pencils and another of red pens. Nothing else, except a carefully folded delivery note.

"Another mammoth crate from S-Cargo," she remarked to Mimosa. "I ordered more than just pens and pencils though; we've nearly run out of photocopier paper."

Before Mimosa had time to reply, Lucy let out a sharp hiss of anger. Mimosa looked up in alarm, thinking this was a warning sign of another episode of COCHRANE or perhaps NOISE, even though there were no chatty library users nearby.

"Those people at S-Cargo must be illiterate, innumerate *and* colour blind!" Lucy exclaimed. "I ordered B pencils, but they couldn't tell H from B, so they've sent us H pencils. Only one box and not two as ordered. Then the pens are red and not black. I knew already they wouldn't supply spiral bound notepads because they've been discontinued unless there is a clinical need, so I didn't even try. But the worst is, they've not sent the photocopier paper I ordered."

Lucy's list of NHS Cargo's misdemeanours was interrupted by Vladimir, who sauntered into the office. "What's the problem, Lu? We've got masses of freebie promotional biros left. I'll get you a couple of boxes from the stationery cupboard."

A very good idea – except that the freebie pens had all dried up. It didn't help Lucy's mood when Simon explained how the S-Cargo employee must have been a foreigner with some musical ability as some countries used a type of musical notation where the note B was known as H. Vlad was the only one who showed some interest in the library manager's learned but somewhat far-fetched theory, so Simon left his staff to sort out their problems and went into the lobby to photocopy a document.

"I should have placed an order before I went on holiday," Lucy said, full of regret. "Now we've got no black or blue pens."

"That *is* a pity, Lucy," Mimosa agreed. "I've just thrown away my last pen, but perhaps we can manage with red pens for a while."

There was a loud groan from Simon in the lobby: the photocopier had jammed again. Vladimir, the only one who could coax the old photocopier back to life, rolled up his sleeves and tackled the machine, but even he had to give up. Lucy put in a call for the engineer, but was told the first possible slot would be in two days' time. "Unless there is a clinical need," Lucy muttered as she put the phone down.

Mimosa had just finished a major printing job and got up to collect it from the printer before producing another document. She opened the paper tray to make sure there was enough paper for her next job, but to her dismay, the tray was empty. She walked over to the broken photocopier, but found only a sheet or two in the tray. What would happen now? This was an important document that had to be submitted as hard copy.

"It's my fault," Lucy repeated, looking very unhappy.

"No, it isn't," Vladimir defended her. "You just said S-Cargo didn't deliver any paper even though you'd ordered some. Anyway, we've now taken an important step towards the paperless office."

Mimosa joined in the conversation, rather annoyed because she would now be unable to carry out her printing. She also pointed out that a library user might come in any moment with a last minute essay to print. They all debated the matter until Simon finally stopped them.

"The important thing in this situation is not to find the culprit, but to think what we should do now. I suggest I go paper rustling in the Trust photocopier room – one ream

48

ought to be enough for any urgent printing jobs. As for pens, that can't be helped."

He disappeared down the corridor. As if on cue, all the lights went out and the computers heaved a sigh and stopped working.

"Oh no!" Lucy wailed. "A power cut is the last thing we want!"

"No pencils, no pens, no photocopier, no paper, no PCs. We'll be reduced to writing with quills and ink at this rate – that is, if Simon can get some paper for us to write on. I'll go and do a bit of shelf tidying in the meantime, there's enough light in the reading room for that," Mimosa said cheerfully. She found the sudden silence quite exhilarating. In the course of the day, one rarely noticed how much the machines whirred and hummed in the background.

There was a flash in Vlad's eyes when Mimosa mentioned quills and ink. It was clear he had come up with an idea. Lucy watched him through the open door as he dived into his desk drawer and broke off a piece from his lunch sandwich, then walked briskly to the window and opened it. A couple of pigeons eyed him with suspicion from a nearby windowsill.

"Come on, Lucy! Put out your hand like this, but really slowly. And remember, right-wing quills for right-handed people," Vlad whispered to his accomplice when she tiptoed to the window.

We shall never know what happened exactly, because it's rude to eavesdrop behind the library manager's door. But the pigeons enjoyed the breadcrumbs, which Vladimir let fall when Simon's hand descended heavily on his shoulder.

SEVEN

CHAIN REACTIONS

Vladimir emerged from his office looking worn out. He had spent an hour and a half on the phone helping Simon Spindrift, a Very Senior (but somewhat computer-phobic) Nurse, access a journal article on My Little e-Library. Vlad's only consolation was that at least the man had now understood that there was valuable information in clinical databases available via the library service, not only on the internet at large.

Lucy hurried to put the kettle on.

"Double hemlock, please. I've just been talking Simon Spindrift through the vagaries of My Little e-Library," said Vladimir wearily and pulled a chair into Lucy and Mimosa's office. "And turn the radiator on, I'm frozen after sitting in my office."

Mimosa looked up from her work. "Skin and bones don't feel the cold," she said with a surprised tone of voice.

"It's not my fault that I don't put on weight like some people," Vlad replied. Simon, who came in at that moment, heard him. "Now don't you two start again," he warned them. "We've got work to do."

"Tell me about it," Vlad grunted. Simon ignored him. "I have some interesting news," he went on. "The Trust is going to have a competition for the best decorated ward or department this Christmas, and I suggest we enter the competition. The first prize is a Christmas hamper."

This kind of work met with immediate approval. The decoration was to be done with as little money as possible, but the library was used to managing on a shoestring budget anyway, so they knew they could cope with that requirement. It was agreed they would set aside a little time each day and then work extra the evening before the jury came.

"Paper chains!" Lucy said dreamily. "I've kept masses of scrap paper from the printouts that people leave behind. We've still got a fortnight, so we can save it all from now on."

"Not much colour," Mimosa pointed out. "But we can add the BMA Library notices, they're always colourful. And anything else that comes in. Maybe we've got a few outdated library guides?" She started leafing through the stationery masters folder in the hope that the perfect Lucy hadn't discarded all of their outdated documents.

"What about the hibiscus in the reading room?" Vlad said. "We could paint the leaves red and pretend it was a poinsettia." To his disappointment, no one thought it was a good idea.

"Snowflakes for the windows would look nice," Simon mused. "We used to cut them out as kids and stick them on."

Lucy reminded him about the bubble wrap. As the old building only had single glazing and the window frames were warped, it was the job of the library staff every winter to cover the worst gaping windows with sheets of bubble wrap, and that meant there was very little pane surface available.

"Never mind, we can take off the wrap the night before and put it back again after the competition. We must decorate at least a few windows for show," Simon said, walking round the lobby assessing the job.

Vladimir surprised everybody by making 3D stars out of four strips of paper for stringing on long threads and hanging on windows. His aunt had taught him to make them when he was a little boy. It was easy to guillotine strips from margins of A4 paper, mostly white of course, but it was agreed that Vlad could use a few strips of coloured paper that they were storing up for the paper chains. A little time was even set aside for the team to learn the new skill, but it was Vlad himself who produced the majority of the stars since he had more experience.

And here is our valiant team on the evening before the event: Vladimir on the library ladder hanging paper chains across the lobby, Lucy cutting a few more snowflakes to put the finishing touches on the windows and glass doors, Mimosa printing out an A3 size poster that said "Happy Christmas to all our customers" to be stuck on the front door, and of course strings of 3D stars hanging on all the reading room windows. Miraculously, a leafy cactus on the reading room windowsill had opened its coral pink buds, so it was placed on the issue desk. Simon was singing "Deck the halls with chains of paper" at the top of his voice even though a couple of readers were still around. The smell of coffee pervaded the library. Who wants a team building day, Simon said to himself – this is the best team building exercise I can think of! And who knew whether this was to be their last Christmas in this location? They would jolly well celebrate it in style.

Suddenly, there was a crash and a roar.

"Samosa, you idiot, look where you're going!" Vladimir yelled. He had moved the ladder so near the reading room that when Mimosa opened the door, it hit the metal ladder and made it rock perilously. Vlad grabbed the top of the nearest journal shelf to steady himself.

"Call me Samosa, and I'll call you Vlad the Impaler!" Mimosa shouted. She was just as shocked as her colleague, but instinctively refused to admit it. Simon hurried to the spot with threaded stars hanging from his fingers and assessed the situation quickly. "Now, don't you two start," he said sternly to Mimosa and Vladimir, who were clearly preparing for a lengthy argument. "We haven't finished our work yet." He cast an anxious glance at Lucy, who was beginning to look a little flaked out. But Lucy smiled at him and continued with her work.

And so in the end all was calm, and they all went home for the night. The following morning, the cleaner was asked to vacuum clean the whole library from top to bottom. The jury entered the moment Adonis had completed his job.

There was a long silence as the jury watched the paper chains and 3D stars moving gently in the draught from the now wrapless windows.

"Beautiful," one of them sighed at last. "I've not seen anything like this since I was a child in the East End after the War."

"Absolutely in keeping with the style of the building," agreed another one.

"What about the budget?" asked the third one, turning to Simon. "Remember you must produce the receipts."

The library manager stifled a smile. "I'm sorry, there are no receipts," he explained apologetically. "Everything was made from scrap materials. Everything, except of course the cactus: that was a present from a library user. Oh, and the poster on the door was printed on new paper."

Yes... The Library Services won the competition, and a colour photo of the team with their winning entry was published in the Trust newsletter.

"Well done, team!" Simon said afterwards as they all sat in the staff room, happily allowing all phone calls to divert to the answerphone. "I'm sure this will bring us new users after the Christmas break."

"It's brought us a Christmas hamper, anyway," Vlad remarked, his mouth full of mince pie.

EIGHT

CLOUDS OVER CARDIGAN BAY

Vladimir woke up suddenly. It was unusually light, and he thought at first he must have overslept. Then he noticed a curious and faint yet familiar smell in the air. He leapt out of bed and pulled the curtains, then dived into the wardrobe. If his colleagues had seen him, they wouldn't have believed their eyes, for Vladimir was smiling. He selected his thickest walking socks, and his heart sang.

***

Lucy rolled over as the alarm clock rang. It was terribly cold. She tried to remember what the weather forecast was for the day, but couldn't. She got up and peered through the curtains, and her heart sank.

***

Not far from Vladimir's house, Mimosa stared out of her bedroom window in dismay. She couldn't believe her eyes as she looked at the massive, bruise-coloured clouds rolling slowly across the sky. What would happen now?

***

In the Pendrives' house, Simon's wife broke the news to him, and he tiptoed downstairs so as not to wake the kids. The situation needed a bit of quick thinking, which was impossible without a mug of coffee.

***

Half an hour later, Vladimir was on the road, marching briskly through the village of Toddling, which appeared deserted. It was about an hour's walk to the hospital in normal circumstances, but today the circumstances weren't normal. Vlad interrupted his whistling as his mobile phone rang. He picked it out of the strap pocket of his backpack.

***

Lucy was ready at last, though she wasn't quite sure whether she was doing the right thing. Should she ring Simon? Didn't the Trust have a policy for this situation? She slipped on her little black shoes and opened the front door, bracing herself for the cold. Within minutes, her fingers were so frozen that she couldn't get her mobile phone out in time to answer when it rang.

***

Cursing under her breath, Mimosa gave up trying to cajole her tiny white car to start. With any luck, she would find a bus; if not, she would simply return home. A bus did in fact turn up hesitantly within a few minutes. As it was slipping along, Mimosa thought she could hear her mobile phone ringing, but she couldn't be bothered to check. There were always mobile phones ringing on buses, and this morning was no exception; in fact that was the only thing that was not out of the ordinary.

***

Simon swore out loud as he tried to ring each of his colleagues in turn, standing in his kitchen. What were the women doing, not answering? What were mobile phones for, if not for staying in touch? Finally, he dialled his deputy manager's number and got a reply instantly.

"Hi, Vlad, it's Simon. I thought you might like to work from home today in the circumstances," he suggested.

"What circumstances?" the other man asked defiantly. "I'm on my way and will be there in ten minutes. You can stay at home if you like." Simon could hear the creaking of Vlad's footsteps in the snow.

"Very well then. I would have liked to come in, too, but my trusty old bicycle..."

"Your rusty old bicycle won't make it," Vlad interrupted. "This is no cycling weather."

He was standing at the library door ten minutes later, stamping his feet to get rid of the rest of the snow; most of it he had already deposited downstairs in the hospital lobby. The door was unlocked, and he saw the staff room door was ajar. How was that possible? He had been sure he was the only one who would brave the elements on a day like this.

He pushed the staff room door open, not sure whether to be pleased or disappointed, and saw Lucy sitting in an armchair, rubbing her feet. A pair of soggy black shoes was perched on the radiator. Vladimir picked the shoes up; on the blazing hot radiator they would dry within a few minutes, but would also curl and harden like a piece of birch bark.

"Melt your butter, burn your leather. That's what my grandmother always says," Vlad said. He dug a plastic bag out of the stationery cupboard, spread it on the floor between the radiator and the coffee table, and placed the shoes on it carefully. Lucy protested. She was shivering and nearly in tears.

"You silly woman, did you really walk here in these? I always thought you were the most sensible one of the lot," he scolded her. "I'll put the kettle on first, and then we'll stuff newspaper in your shoes so they'll keep their shape. Here—"

He handed his furry yellow mittens to Lucy. "Put those on your feet. We can't have you go down with double pneumonia." The girl hesitated. She would look like Donald Duck but furry. A yellow mammoth? An Ice Age version of Donald Duck? But her feet felt so painfully cold that she accepted the offer.

And so it came about that when Mimosa arrived (cross but wearing sensible shoes), Lucy was sitting in the staff room warming her hands around a mug of tea, her feet up to the heels in Vlad's mittens.

Two nurses coming off the night shift dropped in and were impressed to see that the library was staffed. The phone rang, and there was Simon Spindrift, a Very Senior Nurse, wanting an article that was not available electronically on My Little e-Library – and of course he wanted it urgently. He was

58

relieved to hear that the library could fax a photocopy to his home fax.

The phone rang again as Lucy, now comfortable in her office shoes, was copying the journal for faxing. This time it was Simon their manager.

"I've just seen the general email from the Trust office," he told Mimosa. "It seems a lot of departments are closed today, or on skeleton staff only."

"Yes, we've seen that email, too," Mimosa replied. "You'll be pleased to hear there are no skeletons in the library – we're all here. A good thing too, we've had an urgent article request already, plus a couple of readers have shown up."

"Then please send the following email to the Trust office for distribution," Simon said. Mimosa could almost hear him glowing with pride. "'Library services, colon,'" he dictated, "'Business as usual'!"

Vladimir looked out of the window and grinned to himself. More snowflakes were drifting down from the thick mass of clouds. Let it snow – he was prepared for an overnight stay if necessary. He went into his office and shook out the sleeping bag, which had been strapped on his backpack.

NINE

THE KING OF CARDIGAN BAY

Simon was sitting at his desk at home. He was pleased that the other three members of the team had made it to work that day, but right now he was frowning. He had just seen a curious email message, which was written by his deputy librarian and distributed to the health libraries' discussion list, LIS-HELL.

'To all HELL libraries', it read, 'we're pleased to say that it's business as usual at CARB in spite of the twelve inches of snow that surround us. Please do not send us any interlibrary requests though as we're quite busy enough.'

The message was signed by Vladimir Logoff, KING.

***

Something strange was indeed happening at Cardigan Bay. It must have been the strenuous but enjoyable experience of walking all those miles through the snow that had made something go 'click' in the IT librarian's mind. He himself preferred to think that the experience had empowered him. Re-energised him, in fact. Made him find his voice, as they say. Given him a new identity...

It wasn't the first time that Simon had been absent – of course not. But it had never struck Vlad so forcefully before that as deputy librarian he was in charge of the library in Simon's absence.

"KING," he said to himself. "Knowledge and INformation Governor." He sat down and proceeded to amend his email autosignature. Then he got up and looked into Simon's office. Should he move in? It was larger than his own, and the notice on the door stated very clearly that it was the library service manager's office. But Simon's office was draughty when the wind was from the north, as it was at the moment. No amount of bubble wrap could cure that.

Vlad crossed the lobby and entered Mimosa and Lucy's office. They were seemingly busy at their computers, but they were chatting and laughing at the same time. This was not appropriate professional behaviour, the KING decided.

"It's time we had a staff meeting," he said with a firm voice. "Now that Simon is not around, there are a few improvements I'd like to introduce."

There were two dropped jaws in the office. This gave Vladimir time to continue without protest. He straightened his already tall figure to emphasise his height. "The first thing is the untidiness around here," he said, glancing meaningfully at Mimosa's desk. "What are those piles of books, Mimosa? Aren't you supposed to be cataloguing them?"

Mimosa forced herself to answer calmly, squeezing her hands together under her desk.

"The porters brought them in last week. There was no covering letter or compliment slip, so I'm not sure that they're meant to be donations. Some have Brendan Brill's name on them, but..."

"Then the matter is clear, and you should not procrastinate. It says in the procedures manual, Chapter 3 Section 5.1, that all new books, including donations, must be catalogued and processed within five working days of receipt. So, please prioritise this task and pass the books on to Lucy immediately you've finished cataloguing them. Brendan is a library champion, and I'm sure he'd like to see his books put to good use."

Mimosa was speechless with rage. Vlad couldn't possibly quote chapter and verse of the procedures manual, particularly on something that wasn't his job, so he must be making it up. And who did he think he was, anyway, to talk like that? 'Please prioritise this task' indeed!

The KING then found a task for Lucy to carry out urgently – something that completely clashed with what she was in the middle of doing. But Vladimir wouldn't hear any protests; it was best to start the way he intended to continue. "If you don't show more team spirit and cooperate with my efforts to bring some order into this library, I'll contact Claire," he said coldly.

That was a threat that could not be ignored. Claire Twinsett was Simon's new line manager and the CHOKE (CHief Officer for Knowledge, Etc) for the Trust. She was the formidable woman who had scolded them so unjustly when the Library Services had been moved into the hospital cleaning cupboard. They were only too glad that she had never darkened the doors of the library after it had been restored to its former place.

Mimosa and Lucy decided it was wisest to obey Vlad, at least for the time being. After all, the jobs he had given them were things that had to be done sooner or later anyway,

Mimosa reasoned to herself. It wasn't as if he had asked them to clean and dust the library or to do something else that was definitely not in their job descriptions.

It was very nice of Brendan to donate so many books to the library, Mimosa thought as she worked through the pile to check which titles they already had. He hadn't been around lately, so perhaps he had left the Trust. Perhaps that was why he had decided to get rid of the books? But they were mostly brand new, so why hadn't he kept them himself? The Occupational Therapy department had moved recently and was apparently not yet quite settled in their new location, otherwise Mimosa would have given Brendan a quick ring.

Mimosa began to think more and more of coffee as the pile of unchecked books grew lower and lower. Would Vlad see her from his office and snap at her if she sneaked into the staff room and made herself a mug of coffee? She looked round, but Lucy was not at her desk. What if she made a coffee for Vlad as well? That might keep him sweet. She pushed her chair back quietly and tiptoed into the staff room.

When the coffee was ready and Mimosa had taken an encouraging sip or two, she poured out another mug and took it to the IT Lib—sorry, the KING's office.

Vladimir looked at the mug suspiciously. Why should Mimosa suddenly be so helpful? They were frequently at loggerheads with each other, and she had clearly been very angry when he laid down the law about her cataloguing. He sniffed at the coffee.

"You taste it first," he ordered, pushing the mug back.

***

At last Brendan's donations were ready to be entered onto the catalogue. They were all fairly recently published and all very useful. Mimosa made a note to email Brendan to thank him. She took a sheet of book barcodes, peeled one off from the backing sheet and held it gingerly by one corner with her fingertips. She was about to stick it in the book when an email message flashed into view on her computer screen.

'Please help,' it read. 'A box of books that all belong to me personally were sent to our new offices when we moved last week, but it never arrived at its destination. If anyone knows of the whereabouts of these books, please reply to this email or contact the OT department office on...' The message was signed by Brendan Brill.

The barcode detached itself from Mimosa's finger, floated down and landed on the cover of one of Brendan's books, sticky side down. There was no way Mimosa could peel off the sticker without ruining the book. She jumped up and stormed into Vladimir's office.

**

Half an hour later, Simon received an email marked Important.

'Dear Library Manager,' it read, 'I must lodge a complaint as I've been trying to work in the reading room for half an hour now, but cannot do so because of the noise your staff are making, in spite of my plea for a bit of quiet in the library. They seem to be having a major row. Please can you do something?'

Simon reached for the phone and dialled the number of the Healthscare Library. "Stop that racket at once," he bellowed as soon as Mimosa answered. "I'm trying to work!" With that, he slammed the phone down.

Mimosa turned to her colleagues, her eyes round with fright. "That was Simon," she said, almost in a whisper. "He can hear us!"

Silence fell. They all looked at each other, then returned quietly to their desks. And so ended the brief reign of Vladimir I, KING.

TEN

LOST PROPERTY

"What do Charge Nurses do?" asked Lucy one day, standing at the photocopier in the lobby and copying a journal article that another TENNIS library had requested.

"They charge," replied Vladimir. "Just look at Fiona."

They watched through the glass door as Fiona Fatica, a Charge Nurse, approached at great speed along the corridor that led to the Healthscare Library. She was a very energetic and eccentric lady who always wore something spectacular, always had a cheerful word for the librarians, and almost always left something behind in the library. Lucy had lost count of the memory sticks, lipsticks, shopping bags and printouts (some of them confidential) that Fiona had failed to take with her at the end of her visits.

This time Fiona wore a plain, sober T-shirt and jeans, but she was carrying a white, furry hat or shawl on her arm – something that most hospital staff wouldn't be carrying around on a working day – and pulling a large suitcase on wheels. Vladimir leapt to hold the door open for her as she manoeuvred herself, the furry shawl and the suitcase into the lobby. She then settled down at a PC near the photocopier, where Lucy was still busy with her copying.

"I'd love to be a library assistant," Fiona said radiantly. "It's such a nice little job." Lucy agreed politely because she was too busy to explain to the nurse what, and how much, a library assistant's nice little job actually entailed. "I'm glad the library is still here," Fiona continued, "I've heard you're going to be moved to where the staff canteen is now, is that true?" Lucy began to tremble, but managed to explain to Fiona that no such rumours had reached them and that it would be impossible to fit the library in the space occupied by the canteen.

Fiona's mobile phone rang as Lucy finished her photocopying with shaking hands and returned to her office. When she came back again, Fiona had gone. Lucy was not surprised to see the fur hat on the chair. "Guess who was here just now," she called to Mimosa. "Somebody who left something behind."

"Oh, then it must be Fiona," Mimosa said with a benevolent smile. "I'll take it to Lost Property when I go to lunch. Give it to me." She got up from her desk and stepped into the lobby. Lucy reached out for the hat, which raised its head and emitted a loud meow. Lucy jumped back. At that moment Vlad came out of his office.

"This time, Fiona Fatica's forgotten to take her cat with her," Mimosa mentioned with studied unconcern.

"Hat?" Vlad said. "What's unusual about that?"

The hat meowed again, and the man turned to stare at it.

Lucy's bright eyes suddenly turned even brighter. "Perhaps she meant to leave it here?" she suggested. "She had a huge suitcase with her. She must have been going on holiday. I've always wanted a library cat, ever since I read the book about Dewey the library cat in Iowa. Vlad, couldn't we keep it?"

"We must ask Simon," Vlad reminded her. "Incidentally, why do people always talk about library cats? That's terribly racist, or should I say speciesist? Aren't there any library dogs anywhere?"

The cat had been eyeing them from the chair, apparently waiting for the outcome of the discussion. Now it jumped on to the windowsill and turned its attention to the outside world.

Spring had come to Cardigan Bay. The snow had melted and the plants in front of the hospital looked like boiled vegetables, but new green tips were beginning to appear. Pigeons were cooing volubly and strutting on the library window ledges and the roof of the extension below. The cat thought this was rather nice, particularly as one of the windows was slightly open. It tried to push through.

"I got my wrist slapped when I tried to do that," Vladimir remarked bitterly, remembering how he had tried to catch a pigeon to provide quills for their writing needs. He launched forward and reached for the cat. It turned round and took a swipe at him.

"Ouch! The beast!" he cried, holding his hand. Blood was oozing out of two long cuts. "We're definitely not keeping that animal! Get the first aid kit, somebody!"

Unperturbed, the cat turned its attention to the pigeons again, while Lucy patched up her colleague. "I want to give it a name," she said cheerfully to take Vlad's mind off his smarting hand.

"We don't even know if it's a he or a she," Mimosa pointed out.

"That's easy to check," Vladimir said and approached the windowsill again, determined not to let a cat get the better of him. This time he managed to avoid the swing of the paw, but couldn't complete his mission. "Too much fur," he said. "Let's just call it Furry – or Fury. That's appropriate for its temperament."

They then spent several minutes discussing the respective merits of Fury, Dewey, Felix, Felicity and a few others, while the office telephone kept ringing. Finally Vlad came up with Alog. "The cat Alog," he explained to his puzzled colleagues.

"Daft," was Mimosa's verdict.

The cat jumped down from the windowsill and started wandering around the computer workstations. Lucy was concerned that he might chew the cables and electrocute himself. "Good riddance," was Vlad's curt reply. His hand still hurt. Mimosa was worried that the cat might be looking for a litter tray; the last thing they wanted was a smelly carpet. Then the cat found a slip of paper under the workstation where his mistress had been sitting and started to play with it.

The phone rang again, and this time Mimosa answered. It was Simon.

"What's going on?" the library manager asked. "I've been trying to ring here for at least ten minutes. Are you all really so busy that no one can pick up the phone?"

"I'm sorry, Simon. We are actually faced with an unprecedented situation," Mimosa explained. "What did you want?" She was a little annoyed but tried to sound dignified. Of course they should have answered the phone, but then they *could* all be busy at the same time, in theory at least.

"The meeting is running over time, so I won't be back till after lunch. What's this unprecedented situation? I'm very busy, I can't solve your problems—"

"Don't worry then, we can cope," Mimosa said. Just wait till you get back here, she thought. You'll wish you'd listened... At that moment, Alog alias Dewey alias Felicity appeared at the office door and greeted Mimosa loudly.

"What's that?" Simon said at the other end of the line. "Did I hear a meow?"

"It's all right," Mimosa reassured him with the sweetest of malice in her voice. "You go back to your meeting. Perhaps you've been working too hard again?" And she replaced the receiver without waiting for an answer.

The others had been debating the fate of the cat in the meantime. Who would feed it, and who would pay for the food? Simon would certainly not pay for it out of the library budget. Litter tray – would they take turns cleaning it? What about allergic readers? Lucy tried to explain that such obstacles could be overcome as they'd been overcome in the case of Dewey in Iowa, but Vladimir was adamant.

"No, Lucy," he said, "it's all very well, but we can't do it. I'll get rid of him." He grabbed firmly the unsuspecting Alog who had returned to the scene, and pushed the window wide open. Both women screamed 'no' at the same time. The pigeons scattered in all directions.

"What do you mean, 'no'?" Vlad retorted. "I'll get rid of the critter, and that's that. It'll teach Fiona—"

Lucy had picked up the piece of paper which the cat had been playing with. "Wait, Vlad! Wait!" she said quickly. "Listen to this!" She read out the message: "Sorry I have to rush off. Please look after Alec for me. Back by 11. Fiona."

They all looked at each other. Alec tried to sniff at the piece of paper, but couldn't quite reach it while he was in Vlad's arms. "I expect she dropped the paper, and the cat found it. What a relief. It's nearly eleven o'clock now," Mimosa said.

"Alec. Alog. I told you!" Vlad exclaimed triumphantly. He let Alec slip from his arms onto the floor and fetched an incident report form from Simon's office, but then changed his mind. Scratched by a cat? The Health and Safety officer would never believe that.

ELEVEN

ANASTASIA

Simon was sitting in his office when Jill, the medical secretary from next door, stuck her head in. He was checking his financial statements as his budget seemed to be a little adrift, at least according to the Finance department.

"Hi Simon, isn't Vladimir here today? I would have liked to thank him for sorting out my problem with My Little e-Library. He is really good, isn't he! We'll all miss him when he goes on paternity leave," she said, looking around with curiosity. The library manager's usually tidy desk was covered with piles of paper, and a few sheets were also scattered on the floor. Perhaps he was planning the impending library move that Jill's friend had mentioned to her the other day?

Simon felt as if the chair had been pulled from under him. He had had no idea Vladimir had a wife or a partner or even a girlfriend, let alone that he was about to become a father. Simon felt betrayed. Why should he have to hear this from somebody working in another department?

"Anastasia is such a lovely name," Jill went on, completely oblivious of the fact that Simon's face had turned grey. "I wonder where she's from? It sounds Russian. When is she going to have the baby? I heard she's getting wide in the girth, so it must be soon, though I don't think it was a very nice phrase to use."

What would be the best reaction to show now? Simon was sure he had never thought so quickly. If he showed surprise, Jill would be gratified to be the bringer of news – she was known to be a gossip – but it would reveal the fact that Simon had not been taken into his staff's confidence. If on the other hand he pretended to know all about it, Jill would ask him for more details.

The unfortunate manager was spared the choice when the phone rang, so he excused himself to take the call. After a moment's hesitation, Jill decided to make her exit rather than hang around waiting for the end of the call. She would hear about Anastasia and the baby sooner or later; hopefully sooner, before anyone else.

Never did a phone call come at a better moment, Simon thought gratefully, though he found it hard to concentrate on what Penny from the Finance department had to say. Why should he care if the library budget looked like being £300 overspent? It must be their mistake; according to his calculation, they were £3,000 overspent. The Finance people were always messing things up, whereas the Library Services never did. Never. Anyway, the important thing at the moment was that his deputy manager was going on paternity leave and had kept quiet about it.

After the phone call, Simon shut the door – something he normally never did – and sat for a long time staring into his favourite coffee mug, which was painfully empty. Why had Vlad kept so quiet? Did he want to spring a real surprise on his colleagues? Simon had once or twice heard of men who did that simply to enjoy the sensation they created. Vlad did keep to himself a lot, but... could it be that he didn't appreciate his manager sufficiently to talk about such a major matter as starting a family? That was what hurt Simon more than anything. He tried to think of any hints of girlfriends or partners. Holidays? Had Vlad ever said "we" rather than "I" when talking about his holiday plans? And why had he confided in Jill? Maybe he had dropped a casual remark while discussing the problem Jill had had with My Little e-Library?

Finally Simon got up heavily. "Staggered to his feet," he said to himself, and the phrase gave him some satisfaction. That's what they would have said in novels. "Staggered to his feet," he repeated with a grim smile. He called Mimosa into his office and explained what had happened, looking keenly at her to assess her reaction whilst trying not to show his own feelings. *She knew.* All right then, Simon thought bitterly, he has told her but not me, even though they're always arguing. What's wrong with me then? But Simon Pendrive (stress on the second syllable) came from a long line of illustrious librarians, who must have been through similar bitter experiences. Even worse, perhaps. He would bear this humiliation with dignity.

"Oh, Simon!" Mimosa burst out laughing as soon as Simon had finished. "Jill must have overheard my telephone conversation with Vlad yesterday. You know I had to ring him about an urgent problem with Massimo Terremoto's literature search even though he had the afternoon off? Well, he happened to mention that Anastasia was looking potbound and..."

"Hold on!" Simon's voice rose almost to a shout. "What do you mean, potbound? How can you say—"

"No, you've got it all wrong! Calm down!" Mimosa pleaded, fighting to suppress her amusement. Poor Simon. She had better not laugh again. "Don't you remember we gave Vlad a plant for his birthday last year, and he said he would call it Anastasia? Apparently it's grown so vigorously that it needs to be re-potted, and I said, Anastasia must be getting wide in the girth—"

Simon sank back in his chair. What a relief. One of these days he would have a good laugh, but not just yet. Right now, he needed a very large coffee and a bit of thinking time. "Perhaps we won't tell Vlad about this?" he suggested to Mimosa. "I feel a bit silly."

"Don't worry," Mimosa said reassuringly. "You must have had quite a shock when you heard about Vlad's paternity leave, and from Jill of all people. It's not the sort of thing you want to hear from another department."

Simon looked at her gratefully, then got up - not staggering, now - and strode to the staff room. "All's well that ends well. I'll make some coffee," he said over his shoulder.

"Make one for me, too," Mimosa called after him. "And as for Jill, we'll give her a wide girth, I mean a wide berth, from now on."

Simon swung round as if stung. "Birth?!"

"Go and make that coffee now," the assistant librarian said calmly.

TWELVE

THE COFFEE MACHINE

The staff of Cardigan Bay Healthscare Library were gathered solemnly in the staff room around a large, shiny cardboard box, which stood on the corner table next to the kettle. The great moment had come: their coffee machine had finally been delivered by NHS Cargo after two months of waiting. It had certainly done the rounds; the crate that it arrived in was plastered with notes saying NOT KNOWN AT THIS ADDRESS: TRY... and the name of a department. The most remote guess was the Catering department at Backwater Health Centre. Logical in a way, was Vladimir's opinion, since the Catering department catered for people's need for coffee as well as for food.

Simon thought back to the time when he had first tried to order the machine. To start with, he had been told by the most junior member of the Supplies team that he was not authorised to order anything. It had taken him several angry phone calls to discover that the Finance department had recently had an overhaul of the procurement authorisation system and had in the process quite accidentally deleted the Library Services from their list. Equally accidentally, they had forgotten to inform the library manager about the omission.

When peace was restored and the relevant library staff members back on the authority list, Simon received an email from the most junior of the junior members of the Supplies team, informing him that a coffee machine was a non-essential item and he was thus not allowed to order one. This was a new Trust policy.

More phone calls.

"It's my budget," Simon thundered down the line. "I mean the library's. I'll contact my line manager. I'll contact the CEO. I'll contact..."

Mimosa worked out that five large cups of instant coffee were needed before the matter was sorted out and Simon had calmed down – and that was just what Simon himself consumed, never mind his team members who had to support him in his efforts. After that, he still had to create the order on the electronic procurement system, which took him the best part of two hours. Under normal circumstances Lucy would have been told to create the order, but Simon felt that the matter was too delicate to be entrusted to the library assistant, especially one who didn't drink coffee herself.

Then there were the long weeks of waiting, with alternating anxious and angry problem reports faxed to Supplies to query the non-delivery. But here it was at last – the ExasPro coffee machine, Model 007, with an animated display (whatever that was). For an enhanced experience, HazBean coffee was strongly recommended. The only team member who looked a little sad was Lucy, who was on strict orders to regulate her caffeine intake in case she succumbed to COCHRANE again.

Mimosa was concerned because she had bought a packet of Costa Mucho coffee, not knowing about the recommendations of the ExasPro manufacturers. What if Costa Mucho clogged the filter or something? Would they have to call the Estates to sort it out, or would they be able to solve such a problem themselves?

"Don't cross the bridge till you get to it," Vladimir advised her. "We've not even set the machine up yet. I expect it will be my job, or Simon's."

Mimosa's eyes flashed. "Why should it be one of you men? Women are every bit as good with machines as men. I don't see why you—"

"Calm down, Mimosa," Simon said firmly. "I want a cup of coffee, not an argument. And if you, Vladimir, had completed your mandatory equality and diversity training, you would talk more sensibly about gender roles. We'll toss a coin and choose two of us to set up the machine while the others look after the library."

An animated display of staff relations was thus avoided. The lot fell on Mimosa and Simon, who started by reading the instructions. There was a reference to an e-learning package on the manufacturer's website, but they were too impatient for that. Simon filled the jug with water and poured it into the middle of the apparatus, which seemed to be what the tiny picture indicated. The water ran through and on to the hotplate (a good job they hadn't switched the machine on yet), but Mimosa had a paper towel handy, having snatched the last one from the ladies' toilet. Then she rummaged in the stationery cupboard until she found the magnifying glass.

"Where is the reservoir?" Simon wondered. "If you look at the picture, the arrow clearly points to the middle."

They studied the picture again, this time with the magnifying glass, poured more water into the machine, dried up the puddle again (more paper towels, this time from the men's toilet), and came to the conclusion that they were wrong.

"Perhaps we should do the e-learning after all?" Mimosa ventured. Simon was usually in favour of any learning packages that he could persuade his staff to take up.

"E-learning be blowed," Simon fumed, peering into the machine. It was all black and shiny, but in the back of the machine Simon could distinguish a curved empty space that resembled a moat. He filled the jug once again and emptied it into the moat. The water stayed there, and the water level indicator on the side rose gracefully to show Level 0.6. Mimosa was suitably impressed, but there was a further bridge to cross.

"Of course we don't know whether 0.6 means pints or litres. The jug has a different measuring system from the machine itself, it goes from one to ten. That must be cups. How are we going to work this out? Should we ask Vlad? He is good with figures," Mimosa suggested, though she had a sneaky suspicion that Level 0.6 might refer to the level required for successfully completing the e-learning module.

"Vlad be blowed," Simon growled and then corrected himself. "I mean I'm sure you and I can work it out. Let's empty the machine and measure the water with a cup."

Easier said than done. They didn't have a suitable implement for reaching into the deep and narrow moat inside in the machine. Mimosa's suggestion that they should borrow a vacuum cleaner from Adonis was turned down with horror by Simon. He pointed out that if the vacuum cleaner broke down during such an unusual task, they would have to provide a new one from the library budget, and perhaps even do the ordering themselves on NHS Cargo. Mimosa shivered at the thought and agreed with her manager.

In the end they decided the best way to empty the reservoir was simply to up-end the machine and hold it over the waste bin. Mimosa was afraid that Adonis wouldn't like the large wet patches on the carpet, but Simon reminded her that it was only clean water and that they had managed to get most of it into the bin, where a piece of orange peel was now floating merrily.

The calculator was brought out, and after a few attempts Mimosa and Simon agreed about the results of their calculations. The correct measures were then marked on the side of the jug with a permanent marker. The yearning for a cup of real coffee was mounting, tempers were rising by the minute, and it didn't help that Vladimir put his head round the door and asked how they were getting on.

The water was measured. The coffee was measured. Mimosa pointed out the warning on the packaging, which stated that the coffee would be hot.

"I should hope so," Simon snorted, looking round to find something he could wipe his wet shoes with. They had used the last paper towels from the men's toilet now, and Adonis was nowhere to be seen. "Those instructions are meant for idiots, not people like us," he added. A delightful smell of coffee began to spread into the library. Two readers lingered by the staff room door, perhaps hoping to be invited in.

"I think I'll have just a very small cup," Lucy said when her colleagues announced at last that the coffee was ready. "A very small one. I'm sure it's safe, provided I don't eat any chocolate with it. Please, Simon..."

And Simon relented. After all, who had heard of anyone having COCHRANE three times?

THIRTEEN

THE MAN IN THE GREY SUIT

The library services manager of Cardigan Bay Healthscare Library was in trouble. He had been told to cut back on staffing and serial costs in his new budget, and he had achieved this by putting down his staff as pencil sharpeners and journals as post-it notes. Now the suspicious Finance department had called him to a meeting at headquarters. He only hoped he could somehow convince the finance manager that he was suffering from FINES (FINancial Excesses Syndrome).

With a sigh that was meant to break his team's hearts, Simon said goodbye. "I may be some time," he predicted grimly. As he walked out, no one noticed a small man in a grey suit who slipped into the reading room...

There was nothing the team could do to help Simon, of course. They did feel sorry for him, and also rather worried about what might happen to him. "Worst case scenario, they'll sack him," Vladimir said gloomily. He chose not to remember all those times when he had been hauled over the coals by Simon; a known manager is better than an unknown one.

At least they should all get on with their work, Mimosa thought and pulled the pile of new books closer. She would catalogue them before putting the coffee on. She wished ardently she hadn't purchased that book on the history of group therapy in the dental practice, because she had no idea how to classify it. She swore that from now on she would only purchase books she could classify easily. If only another TENNIS library had already held a copy! Then their cataloguer would have been the one to classify it, and she, Mimosa, could have simply added the CARB copy on the shared catalogue.

Vladimir felt restless at his desk and decided to have a look at that difficult computer in the reading room. There was only one library user there, who must have entered while they were busy saying goodbye to Simon. Vlad thought he hadn't seen the man before; perhaps he was one of this month's batch of new employees.

The man looked up from his PC when Vladimir entered. "High time, too," he said in a disapproving tone. "I tried to ring the library before coming here, but I gave up because I had to wait so long. Now I've been sitting here for ten minutes trying to make this computer work."

"I'm sorry, we didn't know you were here," Vlad said. "Let's look at it then." The screen was black and none of the little lights were on. Strange – Lucy had switched on all the computers that morning as per usual and had reported no faults. It didn't take Vlad long to find the fault though: the PC was unplugged.

"What sort of service is this?" the man snorted. "All your computers ought to be on by now."

"I quite agree," Vlad said, trying not to grind his teeth too audibly. He turned to the ancient computer he had wanted to look at, hoping that the awkward customer would attend to his own work. But the peace didn't last very long, because the man quickly checked the library catalogue online (ah well, at least he is computer literate, Vlad said to himself) and wanted to know who had taken out the only loan copy of a book he wished to consult urgently.

Vlad pointed out that they were not allowed to disclose the identity of borrowers. This didn't satisfy the man at all, but Vlad was adamant. At last the visitor accepted Vlad's offer of the photocopying facility since they did have a reference copy in place. The only snag was that the man expected to have the copies made for him, and persuading him to do his own copying took a long time. Appealing to library policy made no impression on him.

As Mimosa got up at last to put the coffee on, she noticed a strange man standing by the photocopier and looking very cross. She was aware that for the last hour or so, she had been hearing the steady chuntering of the machine in the background but it had now stopped, so presumably the machine was out of paper.

"What's the matter with this photocopier?" the man said. "I've been standing and working here for an hour – doing my own copying, mind you – and suddenly the machine stops! You ought to look after your machinery a little better."

Mimosa checked the tray. How was this possible? They had topped up the tray that morning, and now it was empty. A whole ream gone! She bent down to replenish the tray before replying.

"We do look after our machinery, but the tray was empty. If you've been making copies from this book for an hour, then by now you must be in breach of copyright law. Haven't you read the poster?" She pointed to the poster by the photocopier, which detailed what was permitted within the law.

"I'm not interested in your posters. No one cares about copyright law anyway," the man said, but didn't resume his copying. Mimosa slipped into the staff room before anything else could interrupt her mission to the coffee machine. Why did things always happen when Simon was absent? She remembered Fiona Fatica's cat; they had had to deal with that unexpected situation without the manager.

In the meantime, the cross little man made his way to Lucy and Mimosa's office, where he asked Lucy why the journal articles that he had ordered the previous night hadn't been delivered yet.

"I put the interlibrary request slips in the box outside. You must have found them. Isn't that what the box is for, to be emptied every morning?" The man directed a laser glance at the perplexed library assistant. What did he mean by the box outside? She had checked the returns trolley that morning – which could be described as a box since it was cubical – but there hadn't been anything remotely like a bundle of interlibrary request forms in it. She was relieved to see Mimosa back in the office; it was always best to have a witness in these situations.

Before Lucy had time to reply, Mimosa took over. "Let's go and check once more," she said firmly. "You can show me exactly where you put your requests." She took the returns trolley key and led the man into the corridor outside the front door of the library, where he waved his hand in the direction of the tall recycling bin and not the returns trolley.

"That's where I put them, and I demand to know why they have not been processed. They were all urgent."

Mimosa bit her lip and took a deep breath, trying to control the sarcasm in her voice as she explained how the forms would be processed if they were posted in the recycling bin. Unfortunately, Adonis had already done his cleaning rounds that morning, so there were no forms to be retrieved when Mimosa looked into the bin.

"It's a scandal!" the man said indignantly as they returned to the office, where Vlad had also appeared and had been comparing notes with Lucy. "Do you know who I am?"

"No, we don't, because you're not displaying your staff badge," was Vlad's quick reply.

"Staff badge, indeed! I'm Victor A. Moose!" The man cast a triumphant glance at the three librarians, but his name didn't make the wished for impression. Instead, Vladimir asked him whether he worked for the Trust.

"Of course I work for the Trust!" The man's blood pressure was rising visibly.

No sign of recognition flickered in the librarians' eyes. Who on earth was Victor A. Moose, employee of the Trust, who expected them to recognise him? They exchanged glances that said: this is a rogue caller, we should alert Security.

Vlad was about to turn and go into his office to make the phone call, when they heard the front door open and – what a relief – Simon's voice, then a high-pitched female voice, which Lucy was sure she had heard somewhere before. A tall woman stepped into the office, accompanied by Simon.

"Hello, everybody," he said cheerfully. "This is Claire Twinsett, my line manager. I believe you've met her before."

Of course, Lucy thought. She did remember now. This was the unpleasant lady who had reprimanded them for taking over the cleaning cupboard when the library had been accidentally moved there, and who had never revisited them after their return home.

Simon looked and sounded all right, Mimosa thought. His interview with the Finance department must have gone well after all. And now he could take over this awkward customer.

Damn it, Vladimir thought. I was enjoying the battle with that guy, and now Simon will sort him out instead.

Claire Twinsett smiled and turned to the mysterious man, who also smiled. "I must explain my presence," he said and inclined his head courteously. "I'm Claire's PA, and I was sent here to gauge the library's response to a difficult customer – a mystery shopper, in other words. The committee that deals with the Team of the Month award has received so many nominations for the library team that we became quite intrigued, and it was Claire's idea that we should test you."

Simon looked alarmed. How had they tested his team? How had they performed? He imagined Vlad's curt replies, arguments in front of the visitor, Lucy bursting into tears...

"You all did very well, and the library manager can be proud of his team," Victor A. Moose said, smiling even more widely. "We'll be very happy to support your nomination."

"In that case, wouldn't you two like to stay a bit longer? I've just made a fresh pot of coffee," Mimosa suggested. There was no harm in showing that their good manners had not been lost by their testing experience.

A pot of coffee? Claire Twinsett frowned. How come the library had a coffee machine? It did not count as an essential purchase. Perhaps she should look into Simon's budget again on her return to headquarters...

FOURTEEN

THE BOMB

Lucy heard the sound of an incoming text message and picked up her mobile phone. She read the brief message and turned to her colleague in utter disbelief.

"Mimosa," she said faintly, "you won't believe this, but I've just received a text message from Vlad saying there is a bomb in the library. Listen: *Bomb in lib at noon. Search!*"

Vladimir had the morning off, so goodness knows how he had discovered this horrifying piece of information. But this was not the time to wonder about Vlad's source of information; they would find out afterwards – if there was an afterwards, Lucy thought.

"I can't believe it," Mimosa said with determination. "Ring him and ask him what he means. We won't alert Simon until we hear a bit more."

Lucy wasn't sure that Mimosa was right. The library manager ought to be informed immediately, and so should Security, and what about evacuating the library? But she did as she was told, since Mimosa was her senior. She tried once, she tried twice, but Vlad's phone was turned off.

It was a quarter to twelve.

When Simon heard the news that a bomb had been planted somewhere in their library, he took it marvellously calmly. In his heart of hearts, he experienced a quick surge of joy; how many of his ancestors had been confronted with such a serious situation? But this was something he could not share with his staff; it would have to wait until he got home to his wife – if he ever did, he thought.

"Just a minute, I'll find my disaster management plan," he said and turned to his computer with a flourish. But unfortunately he had not yet covered the possibility of bombs in his plan, so they had to improvise.

"Never mind about finding the bomb," he said to Lucy, who was peering fearfully into the coffee machine. "We must evacuate the library, and the police will then send a special unit to carry out a search."

Mimosa reminded him how difficult it was to evacuate the library when the fire alarm sounded as most people simply carried on with their work, but Simon said grimly that the word 'bomb' ought to make the blighters move.

There were no readers in the library. Thank goodness for that, Lucy thought, as she wrote out a large notice to put on the door.

"You can't write that," Mimosa protested. "Saying there is a bomb in the library is bad policy. They'll never come again!"

"But they must be told why we're closed," Lucy insisted. "You can't just say 'staff training', can you?"

"Of course you can," Mimosa replied coldly. "Much more dignified." Lucy tried to tell her that there might be no library for readers to come back to if the bomb went off, but Mimosa didn't listen. She picked up the phone and dialled the number for Security, only to hear the following message: *The Security service on site has been discontinued. Please turn to the*

Human Resources department if you need help. In urgent cases, dial the number for the hospital Reception.

Precious minutes were lost when Simon wanted to listen to the answerphone message himself. It simply beggared belief that the Security service had been discontinued without prior warning. At last he gave up and dialled the number for Human Resources. He was aware of the minutes ticking away, but forced himself to keep calm. The image of his ancestors flitted briefly through his mind again, but it was a distraction that he didn't want to dwell on. Afterwards, he thought – if there was an afterwards.

We're unable to answer your phone call today, the automated voice announced politely, *as the Human Resources department is having an away day. If your problem is urgent, please hold the line and our clerical assistant will be with you shortly.*

The clerical assistant, however, didn't know anything about security. "They only asked me to be here to answer the phone," he said defensively. "They didn't say anything about giving out information, they just went off to have their away day and left me here. Anyway, information about security might be confidential for all I know."

In the meantime, Mimosa had taken the step of phoning Reception and demanding that they send for the person responsible for security. After she was told that there was no such person on site any longer and that it would take at least half an hour to get one over from Backwater, Mimosa took a deep breath and disclosed the fact that they had been told there was a bomb in the library.

"In that case, you should ring the Estates and log a call. Have you got the number?" the receptionist said, polite as ever.

Mimosa cast a glance at Lucy, who was behaving very bravely considering her delicate nerves and gathering together what she regarded as their most valuable possessions: a copy of the first edition of *Diseases of the Left Nostril* from the shelf where the historical collection was housed, an armful of books on loan from other libraries... what else? Lucy went into the staff room and hesitated. Would the coffee machine count as valuable? Simon had spent ages trying to order it and then setting it up with Mimosa, so in terms of staff time it was probably quite high on the list of valuables. Then she decided against it as it was too heavy and unwieldy, and returned to the office where Mimosa was still on the phone, this time to the Estates.

"We don't have any instructions about removing bombs, so it's not a routine job," the Estates clerk explained to Mimosa, who had miraculously succeeded in getting through at first attempt. "You must fill in a New Works form and ask your manager to sign it. Then fax it to us and we'll assign a priority number to it. At the moment it's likely to be Priority 3 as we're experiencing an unprecedented—"

At this point, Mimosa began to tremble in an unprecedented fashion and put the phone down, not very delicately. Simon could hardly wait to hear what she had been told, which she somehow managed to repeat coherently.

It was three minutes to twelve.

"Never mind," Simon said comfortingly. "Let's get out of here, we're the most valuable asset in this place. I'll make sure I fill in a problem report afterwards – if..." He didn't finish his sentence. He picked up his keys and his mobile phone, ushered Lucy out of the staff room and opened the front door.

As they were about to step out, a library user approached them. It was Anna Achinside, a consultant. "I hope I'm not late," she said. "I was expecting to see Vladimir here; I've booked a literature search with him at twelve."

Simon opened his mouth to explain the situation, but Lucy stopped him. There was suddenly an excited expression on her pale face. She pulled out her mobile phone and began to create a text message, leaving the predictive text function on.

Anna, she keyed in, and the phone obediently changed it to *Bomb*.

FIFTEEN

THE REFLECTIVE PRACTITIONER BUYS A PAIR OF TRAINERS

That had been an eventful morning. Not only did they have to respond to the bomb scare created by Vladimir's thoughtless text message, but Mimosa had also had to do an hour's assisted literature search with Anna Achinside immediately after the alarm had proved false.

Dr Achinside usually reminded Mimosa of the description of a certain cheese: mild, continental, slightly sweet and nutty. But this time the consultant had been in a real state – holding her head, talking slightly incoherently, perspiring – all because her own search had gone pear-shaped and it was tremendously urgent to have the right information for her case conference the following day. She had been immensely grateful for Mimosa's help, almost in tears. So far she had only ever tried to find information on the internet, but now she was finally convinced that she needed to search in clinical databases, only she didn't know how and in fact had never even obtained a username for herself.

"That's all right, that's what we're here for," Mimosa had said in reply. Not that she felt so brilliant herself, having had such a terrible time with the false bomb alarm and then having to help Dr Achinside without a moment's preparation or a coffee break, or any kind of debriefing after the traumatic event.

But now Mimosa had two precious hours off, all to herself, and she was going to spend some of that time finding a pair of decent shoes or perhaps trainers. She really ought to start walking more, she thought. She remembered how exhausted she had felt that day in winter when she had had to walk home through the snow because there were no buses in the afternoon. She had also noticed that her back had begun to protest lately whenever she spent too long at her desk without a break. What's more, she was putting on weight. She thought longingly of the picture of a librarian she had seen in those library stories in *HEL's Bells*; somebody had once said it resembled her. If only! Such a slim and elegant looking character...

Timidly, Mimosa entered the first sports shop she could find. She was embarrassed because sports shops were so clearly for people who were fit and athletic or at least outdoor types. The advertisements showed them posing on top of unscaleable mountains yet looking as fresh as if they had only taken a stroll to the corner shop. Therefore the shop assistants would presumably be the same type, and they would look down on couch potatoes like her.

It was a little reassuring that the first shop assistant Mimosa saw was a young man whose tracksuit didn't quite fit him and whose suntan – a sure sign of outdoor life – had somehow failed to develop. Even better, he immediately became alert when she mentioned her protesting back as well as her desire to start walking more in order to become fit. It turned out that the young man specialised in back problems, so Mimosa began to relax and even forgot her embarrassment.

But alas, things were not so simple. Fourteen boxes and forty minutes later she still hadn't made up her mind about which pair fitted best.

"Take your time," was the young man's advice. "I'll bring you as many pairs as you want. The main thing is you get a pair that you feel comfortable in."

"I think I'd better take a break," Mimosa said feebly. "I'll be back soon." She knew she would have to start all over again because she couldn't possibly remember which pairs were nearly right, but she simply couldn't take it any more without a break.

She headed for her favourite café, ordered a large coffee and a wicked cake and reflected on her afternoon's project. It had never crossed her mind that sales personnel in a sports shop could specialise further. Was it like the library service, then? One of them was in charge of collection management, another one dealt with document supply, the third one was an IT specialist... In a small library they had to be ready to take up any customer services whenever there was a need, yet they all had their own special areas of responsibility, something they could develop further.

Mimosa had recently read a book on how to be a reflective practitioner and was now wondering whether the shop assistant was reflecting on his performance while she was having a coffee. What would he be thinking? And oh dear, she herself had not thought any further about the morning's events. Wasn't there something they should reflect on? She remembered how she had exploded – hmm, perhaps that was an unfortunate word, seeing that they had had a bomb scare – when Vlad walked in and greeted them cheerfully after his morning off.

"It's all very well for you," she had said, shaking with rage. "You've been resting on your laurels while we've been turning the place upside down to find a bomb, just because your lordship couldn't be bothered to check his spelling!"

Poor Vladimir hadn't known what to say. He and Mimosa often had arguments, but usually there was at least some shred of truth in what they flung at each other, whereas now he simply couldn't understand a word of what she was saying. Unfortunately, stating this made matters even worse. Mimosa started yelling at him until he, too, lost his temper and added to the decibels. Then Simon emerged from his office, furious because of the noise.

"I've got a house full of squabbling teenagers, and that's quite enough for me. I don't want to hear arguments at work as well. Now will you two stop, or will I have to SPEAK IN BLOCK LETTERS?"

By this time, Lucy was trembling almost as much as Mimosa. She simply hated it when anyone around her had an argument. Oh, why couldn't they stop? Why did they all have to shout, even Simon? She ran back into her office and slammed the door.

In the end everything was sorted out, hurt feelings salved, Simon had a private word with Vladimir, and Mimosa was asked to amend the section on communication in the Policy and Procedures manual to the effect that predictive texting was not to be allowed in text messaging. So, Mimosa thought – finishing her coffee – had they handled the situation from beginning to end as they should have done? Perhaps she wouldn't have shouted at Vlad if she could have been debriefed after the bomb scare was over, whereas now she had had to provide good service to Anna Achinside and pretend everything was all right. Any other time, she would have thought helping her was simply something in the day's run, and her reply, "That's what we're here for," would have been genuine.

Mimosa returned to the sports shop, where the assistant had piled the boxes up neatly but hadn't taken any of them back to the store. How nice it was to be at the receiving end of good service, she thought with relief. Was this how Dr Achinside had felt after having been helped by Mimosa?

"I've brought another pair for you from the store," the young man said, pulling out one more pair of trainers from a box while Mimosa settled on the bench and removed her shoes. What a lovely colour, she thought. It would be nice to have a pair like that. She pulled them on, stood up, took a few steps and let out a deep sigh. Incredible. They fitted like a glove, and she could feel her back straightening to a comfortable, healthy posture. Suddenly, the world was all right.

She had to swallow twice before she could trust her voice. The young man was still kneeling on the floor and looking up at her.

"They're perfect," she said. "I'll take them. Thank you so much." She had to stop because she knew she would start crying if she said another word.

"That's all right," the young man said. "That's what we're here for."

SIXTEEN

TRY AGAIN, CARDIGAN BAY

"Now the blighters have finally broken the old printer," Vladimir grunted one morning. His manager reprimanded him for accusing the readers so rudely; it sounded as if they had done it on purpose.

"All right then: now the old printer has finally been broken by the blighters," Vlad said stubbornly, leaving Simon wondering about the subtle difference between the two utterances.

"I'm fed up with this place," Vlad went on, throwing himself into the easy chair opposite the manager's desk. "A broken printer as well as a dodgy photocopier. Look at the string that Lucy has tied to the lid to hold it up! It must be a Health and Safety hazard. And what about the walls in the office? Spotted with old Blu-Tack marks."

"I know," Simon admitted, picking up his coffee mug. "We've discussed this more than once. You know as well as I do that there simply isn't that sort of money in the budget, and besides, we may be moved somewhere else within a few months and the Powers That Be won't refurbish a department that's about to move. But I heard this morning that there may be money in the Trust for essential refurbishment – emphasis on 'essential'. Why don't we try to get some of it?"

They went into the staff room, where Simon told Mimosa and Lucy the news. Everybody was suddenly excited. This was their chance! But how bad would things have to be before the refurbishment could be called essential? They dropped everything else they were doing and started looking round for the most glaring faults.

It didn't take Mimosa long to think of something. She brought the sheets of bubble wrap out of storage, and together she and Lucy stuck it in front of the windows, as they usually did for winter.

"Are you mad?" Simon exclaimed when he saw what the ladies were doing. "It's August! They'll never believe we need those. Take them down at once!"

"It can be quite cold and windy in August in this country," Mimosa said calmly, spreading out another sheet. "It's worth the effort if we can convince the inspecting committee of our parlous state. We must all think of something convincing now."

The wallpaper in the lobby was peeling off near the ceiling above the library manager's door. Vladimir brought the library ladder from the reading room, climbed up and tugged at the flapping wallpaper. As a result, the flap now hung gracefully over the door.

Vlad climbed down with a look of satisfaction on his face. He rolled the ladder back into the reading room and turned to survey the old, faded curtains. A tug didn't do much in this case, but when he casually passed a pair of pointed scissors down each curtain, they developed a very convincing shredded look.

Meanwhile, Simon was examining the coffee-stained carpet in the lobby.

"Bad stains, those," he remarked to Lucy, who was in the staff room collecting a ream of paper from the stationery cupboard. Simon poured himself another coffee and left the room. Of course it was a pure accident that Mimosa came in just as Simon was passing Lucy in the doorway, so that Simon's coffee was knocked flying. After that, everybody's verdict was that the coffee stains on the carpet were very bad indeed.

***

"Don't forget that we must clean up here," Simon reminded his team the day before the refurbishment committee was due to inspect the library. "We mustn't give them the idea that we don't look after the place, otherwise they'll never consider our application."

It was therefore hard to believe that when the committee looked into the IT librarian's office, they saw four coffee mugs in various stages of mould growth. Simon glanced nervously at the committee and felt he ought to explain.

"We've recently embarked on an experiment on mould growth in association with the staff canteen. We..." he began.

"That's very interesting," one of the committee members interrupted him drily. "I've been nominated Research and Development Lead for the Trust, but this is the first I hear about such an experiment. Perhaps your application letter hasn't reached us yet."

Mimosa and Lucy's office fared little better. There were cake crumbs on Mimosa's desk, and the committee didn't seem impressed when Lucy explained they were there for the mouse.

Vlad was fuming silently in the background. Damn it, this was not an army sergeant major's inspection! What did it matter if they had mouldy coffee cups or cake crumbs in their offices? This inspection was about the condition of the library, not about details of tidiness. But he kept quiet.

The committee moved into the reading room, where the shredded curtains were gently swaying in the draught. Simon decided to make a speech about the importance of the working environment for staff morale. A nurse had been working at a computer and got up to go, but hit his knee on the edge of the workstation and hissed with pain.

"Sorry about that," Simon said politely. "These workstations aren't really meant for computer work."

"I can see that," the nurse said crossly, rubbing his knee. "This one looks more like an old Singer sewing machine table."

Simon's eyes lit up appreciatively. "You're on the right track," he said. "Only it's a Husqvarna table."

"I'll be on the track of the Health and Safety officer," the nurse muttered and turned to go. The doorknob came off as he tried to open the door.

When the doorknob had been fitted back – the committee watching all the time – and the nurse had departed, Simon started on his staff morale speech again, waxing quite eloquent as he went on. After all, he was Simon Pendrive (stress on the second syllable), descendant of a long line of illustrious librarians, and he knew how to deliver a speech. The curtains fluttered in the draught quite furiously now, and Simon thought he could hear a sob. He realised it was Lucy, who was apparently hiding behind the curtains. That was really too much, Simon thought, biting his lip. He would have to tell Lucy off. What was she doing in the reading room while the visitors were there? Was she eavesdropping on the progress of the visit, or simply trying to create an impression of draught by moving the curtains?

Simon turned the other way so as to lead the committee's attention away from the suspiciously behaving curtains. One of the assessors – the Research and Development Lead – interrupted him and said in his dry voice that they had heard enough. Simon thought the man reminded him of his old Latin master. (*Pendrive, you may have spent the weekend studying the Dewey Decimal Classification, but it's no excuse for not having done your Latin translation again.*)

"When was the library last refurbished?" another member asked.

"There is nothing about it in the hospital archives, and they go back to 1875," Simon said. "This must therefore be the original interior." He stopped to scratch his ankle and apologised. "It's the fleas in this carpet again," he explained. "The cleaner has tried putting flea powder down, but the library users complain it makes them sneeze. Vacuum cleaning helps only temporarily, and of course it wears the carpet out if we have it done any more often. There is already a hole under—"

"Fleas?" the head of the committee repeated with disgust. "That is absolutely abominable. Why haven't you reported this before?"

Simon thought quickly. This time he had gone too far. "Let me see," he said. "I'm sure I reported it once last year, but that must have been when the email system was down. Then I reported it earlier this year, but..."

"Excuses, excuses," said the head crossly. "We've heard enough. You must present your refurbishment plan within eight working days, and we'll find the money. We won't take up any more of your time now."

They turned to go out, and Simon hurried to open the door for them. The doorknob came off again, but this time he didn't bother to fit it back on. The main thing was that the door could still be opened. It was a shame of course that Vlad had treated the doorframe with a sharp object, so that the Research and Development Lead got a splinter in his hand. Mimosa was called in with the first aid kit.

"*Vae victis,*" Simon said to himself with secret satisfaction, watching Mimosa remove the splinter with more vigour than gentleness.

SEVENTEEN

A DESIRABLE LOCATION

The fact that the Healthscare Library had been completely refurbished did not go unnoticed. Some users had heard a rumour that the library's closure was not temporary but permanent, some thought the library had moved, but most of them were au fait with events and returned little by little after the library had reopened. Or, as Vladimir put it, they crept out of the woodwork.

One day soon after the reopening, three very cheerful and very round ladies entered, immediately beginning to utter oohs and ahhs to each other. Simon looked up from the new multifunction device that was supposed to photocopy *and* scan *and* print, though he was still having problems even keying in his password. It was gratifying to hear the ladies' enthusiastic comments, but Simon was sure he had never seen them before. Perhaps they could be invited to join this wonderful, dynamic, freshly refurbished library?

The ladies peered into the office. Simon heard Lucy ask them if she could help, but they withdrew, saying they were "just looking". They then peered into Vladimir's office, and the same conversation was repeated. Simon began to feel a strange tingling in the nape of his neck, as if warning him. What if these ladies were mystery shoppers, like Victor A.

Moose had been? If so, was the team showing sufficient professionalism? On the other hand, if they weren't mystery shoppers, then who were they and what were they doing here? People who simply wanted to join the library didn't usually behave like this.

Having performed a similar brief check on the reading room, the visitors stepped into the library manager's office while Simon was still attending to the misbehaving multifunction device. Drat it, he thought, this isn't even a unifunction device at the moment!

"This looks about right," he heard one of the ladies say. He turned round in alarm and stepped across the lobby to meet them.

"You must be the manager," the most cheerful looking lady said to Simon, who of course was gratified to have been instantly recognised. "This space looks wonderful, and we'd like to have the reading room for the use of our department."

Simon cast a quick glance at the lady's well-shaped bosom, but there was no staff badge to be seen. Oh dear, definitely another mystery shopper... The other two weren't wearing any badges, either.

"I'm afraid the reading room is for the use of library members. Moreover, my line manager has not mentioned any plans to reallocate it to another department," Simon explained, cool but polite, though beads of perspiration were beginning to gather on his forehead. Three mystery shoppers would be vastly preferable to another unannounced move, or (worse still) having to share their space with another department. Could it be that Claire had somehow failed to keep him in the loop?

"Well, could we have your office then?" another member of the trio suggested.

I'd better laugh, Simon thought, because this must be a joke. He tried, but his laughter sounded more like a menacing croak.

"Just joking," the third lady said hastily, glancing at her friends. "We'd like to join the library, actually. And I must say it does look very nice here. Very impressive!"

Simon showed the visitors to Lucy and Mimosa's office and retired into his own office, his heart beating rapidly. Why could the NHS not allow employees a bottle of whisky in the desk drawer for situations like this? Just joking, indeed! A manager's office was his castle.

It was Vladimir's turn next to receive a shock. He was alone in the reading room, crawling on the floor to replug a computer, when two very serious and very tall men in dark grey suits entered.

"No one here, as usual," one of the men remarked. "That's what I thought all along; nobody uses the library," the other one chimed in. "Wasting money on refurbishment! We should have waited until another department moved in."

At that, they left. Vlad emerged from under the workstation with such haste that he banged his head against it, thus losing a few precious seconds. By the time he had got up and followed the men, they had already disappeared into the corridor.

He went in search of Simon, but the manager had gone to the café to regain his peace of mind. Vlad told his colleagues what had happened.

"Oh no!" Lucy moaned. "It was bad enough with those three ladies Simon had to deal with."

"This is now what is known as a desirable location," Mimosa said. "But it makes me feel threatened. Remember how they accidentally moved us into the broom cupboard?"

No one could have forgotten that traumatic experience. They looked at each other. Simon was downstairs in the café, and there was no knowing when the next caller would come and challenge them. But before they could think of an action plan, Fiona Fatica, Charge Nurse, appeared.

"Hello, all," Fiona chirped. She put down the large basket she was carrying and fanned herself with her hat. "You look very gloomy on such a nice day in such a nice library! Why is that?"

They explained. "What we really need is a guard dog," Vladimir added. "The intercom doesn't help when people can use their access badges or simply tailgate others."

"How about a cat?" Fiona suggested, opening the basket. "How about Alec?"

A furry white face peered out. Of course they all remembered Alec, the cat that Fiona had once left behind. He really was whiter and silkier than a cat had any right to be. Lucy and Mimosa uttered oohs and ahhs not unlike the ones that the nice round ladies had uttered earlier about the library, but Vlad was suspicious. He hadn't forgotten how Alec had sunk a pawful of sharp claws into his hand.

"Believe me, he is a remarkable cat," Fiona continued. "If you say 'what's this?'" – here she lowered her voice into a whisper so as not to alarm Alec – "he'll attack you. He can't stand that phrase."

"No, I don't believe it," Vlad admitted. "But it does sound useful. We could scare away any callers who threaten our existence. That is, if you let us borrow Alec. Trouble is we're not sure how long this may continue."

Trouble is, Mimosa thought, that Simon will never agree to such a plan. We want to encourage people to use the library and not to scare them away, he would say. Besides, was it really possible that a cat would react to a couple of words so strongly? Wasn't it rather the tone of voice? And would he in fact attack so furiously as to make an unwelcome visitor turn, erm, tail?

After a brief discussion, they decided that their practice ought to be evidence based. Fiona therefore coaxed Alec to sit on the windowsill in the lobby, and Lucy and Vladimir stayed nearby, curious to see the outcome of the experiment. Mimosa refused to participate, saying somebody would have to look after the office. Fiona settled by a computer to check her emails.

They didn't have to wait long. Lucy had only just finished tidying up the photocopying area and Vlad was trying to talk nicely to his old enemy, when Simon returned. He had bought a sandwich to take back to the office, so he was now walking along the corridor, viewing his prawn sandwich in anticipation and talking to Simon Spindrift, a Very Senior Nurse.

"I can smell that sandwich," the nurse remarked. "Good job there are no cats around, otherwise they would all be following you."

They laughed. Simon Pendrive said goodbye to the other Simon (who had come to visit a consultant whose office was in the library corridor) and opened the library door.

Well, I'm blowed, the library manager thought, frowning. What's that heap of fur on the windowsill? And why is Vlad standing idle when he has deadlines to meet? He stepped briskly to the IT librarian. "What's this?" he demanded sternly. "What's this?"

Alec, on cue, leapt from the windowsill with an angry hiss and straight onto the unsuspecting Simon's shoulder, sinking his claws in for balance. The man let out a yell and tried to rescue his sandwich packet, but it slipped and the contents fell out.

"I told you!" Fiona exclaimed triumphantly. "There is your evidence! Oh, you clever puss!"

Alec ignored his mistress's praise. The only reward he was interested in was that delicious-smelling sandwich, which now lay on the floor without its container.

EIGHTEEN

HOOKED!

"That coat on your chair back looks untidy," Simon remarked to Mimosa one morning. "And the same thing with yours, Lucy. Can't you hang them up?"

"No, we can't, we lost our coat hook in the Great Refurb," Mimosa explained ruefully.

It was true. The Healthscare Library had been thoroughly refurbished with new carpets, paint, curtains, workstations – everything, except for one small item: the coat hook behind the door of the library office had been removed by the painter and never put back.

"Do you really need one?" Simon wondered. "You could keep your coats in the staff room, out of sight."

"It's better to have them here. I'll order a hook from NHS Cargo," Lucy said. "Quite simple."

Famous last words... Ordering anything unusual from S-Cargo was not a simple matter, as she remembered after spending forty minutes searching for a coat hook in the online catalogue. She mustered all her search skills and tried to think of synonyms, near synonyms, opposites and likely misspellings, but she couldn't find anything even remotely resembling a small object that was slightly curved at one end and fastened to a wall or a door at the other, and to which one could append one's coat.

"Let me try," Mimosa said. As a qualified librarian with advanced search skills and long experience, she was sure she would succeed where Lucy had failed. But S-Cargo defeated her, too. In the end, they rummaged in the staff room and found an old paper copy of the catalogue, where the desired object could be located easily. The only snag was that the smallest quantity one could order was two dozen. Lucy tried phoning other departments in case anyone else wanted a coat hook so they could share the order, but it was no use. She gave up when Dr Achinside's secretary pointed out that she would probably not be allowed to order coat hooks anyway since they would be deemed unessential – nor was there a clinical need, Lucy added to herself.

They decided to drop the matter and do as Simon had suggested. The first autumn rains came, and both ladies spread their wet overcoats in the staff room to dry.

"Not very nice," was Vlad's comment. "You can't sit down anywhere without getting soaked. Why can't you keep your coats in your office?"

"It's all very well for you to talk," Mimosa retorted, "you've got two coat hooks in your office. Perhaps we could remove one of them and have it fixed on our door?"

But Simon, who overheard the discussion, was against this plan. "You can't remove a hook without leaving a mark, and we're not going to have marks in the nice new paint," was his managerial verdict.

They then discussed suction cup hooks, but dismissed the idea as they wouldn't be strong enough. "I'll buy a coat hook for you on my way home today," Simon promised in the end.

That made him feel really good about himself. Just the sort of thing a manager ought to do for his staff, he said to himself, rubbing his hands together. And such a simple solution, too. Why hadn't he thought of it before?

After visiting three shops, where they only sold coat hooks by the dozen or else elaborate six-hook affairs, or had never heard of coat hooks, Simon began to feel his halo pinching a bit. I'm blowed if I'm going to spend the afternoon hunting for a coat hook, he said to himself. One more shop, and then I'll give up.

Of course it was the last shop that sold coat hooks singly, or by weight, or whatever the customer wanted. A good old fashioned ironmonger, such as you rarely saw these days. The assistant put the hook in a small brown paper bag and issued Simon with a carefully written out receipt as requested. Simon pocketed his purchase, folded the receipt solemnly and put it in his wallet.

The following morning, he dropped in at the cashier's on his way upstairs. Since the coat hook was a purchase for the library, he felt justified in getting his money back from petty cash. He approached the counter and produced the receipt.

"I'm sorry, but we no longer pay back from petty cash," the cashier explained. "We only deal with patient finances now. You should have ordered your coat hook through S-Cargo."

Never mind, Simon said to himself. He was Simon Pendrive (stress on the second syllable), the descendant of a long line of distinguished librarians, and he should have known better than to ask for reimbursement for such a trivial little item. The main thing was that he had done the right thing for his staff.

The coat hook was welcomed with jubilant cries. "Now we must have it fixed on the door," Lucy said. "I'll ask Al from the Estates, I saw him working in the yard just now."

She opened the window and called out to Al Monte, explaining what was wanted. Unfortunately, Al shouted back that fixing a hook on a door counted as Minor Works, so he couldn't simply come up and do it.

And now you have several witnesses to your conversation, Mimosa thought; two or three other men working around the yard, one of them the Estates manager. So, definitely no chance of persuading Al to do the job without paperwork; they all knew that Mr Moore-Gubbins was a stickler to the rules.

Lucy sighed and sat down to fill in a Minor Works form. Simon authorised it duly, but with a slight frown.

"We have more important things to do than filling in forms," he remarked, choosing not to tell Lucy how much time he had spent trying to find an ironmonger that sold coat hooks. Lucy of course was glad she had never told Simon how much time she and Mimosa had spent on searching for the hook on S-Cargo's electronic ordering system.

"Those coats really do look untidy when you hang them on your chairs," Simon added. "I'm glad we'll see the end of this business soon."

Three rainy days and three times two wet coats later, Al turned up. But no one could remember where the hook had been stored. Mimosa was sure Vlad had picked it up and used it for his own purposes, Lucy blamed herself for not looking after it, and Simon was getting more and more cross about the Never-Ending Expenditure of Time. In the end he found the hook in his desk drawer. Meanwhile, Al had been waiting patiently. Now Mimosa pointed out the office door to him, and she and Lucy decided to do some shelf tidying in the reading room in order to be out of the way.

It didn't take long before Al called the ladies back into the office. There it was, the long wished for hook, on the outside of the door.

"It's very nice, Al, but we actually wanted it on the inside, to hang our coats on," Lucy explained, seeing that Mimosa was speechless with fury.

"How was I to know?" Al defended himself. "It says on my job ticket: *fasten hook on library office door*. This is the library office, isn't it? And this is the door. When the door is closed, this is the side you see first, so of course I fixed the hook there. Yes?"

Much to his annoyance, Al had to remove the hook and fix it on the inside. But his annoyance was nothing compared to Simon's, when he saw the ugly mark on the new paint. He insisted that Al should make good the job, but when he heard it would take at least three weeks because Estates were short staffed, he relented.

"Never mind," he said. "But make sure you do come and do it without us having to fill in another form. For now, we'll put up a poster to cover the mark."

It's best not to describe Simon's reaction when he discovered that removing the poster took several pieces of paint with it. He calmed down eventually and admitted that the main thing was that Lucy and Mimosa now had a hook for their coats. But come to think of it – shouldn't they have asked for a hook each while they were about it?

NINETEEN

BUSINESS AS USUAL?

Vladimir did not forget the two tall and serious men who had come in on a quiet day soon after the refurbishment and had drawn the conclusion that no one used the library. They were wrong – so wrong – but how could he prove that? The memory rankled in Vlad's mind. Everybody knew that they were busy; everybody except some idiotic visitors who clearly believed that the library ought to look like the centre of town at the beginning of the Boxing Day sales.

One Friday afternoon, Simon mentioned to Vlad that they ought to try out the broadcasting functionality of the library management system. This was a convenient way of emailing a selected group of users in one go. Vlad listened attentively as Simon explained how the broadcast was to be sent to all library users whose membership had expired, inviting them to update it.

"Sounds good," the IT librarian commented. "They can respond in person or by email or by phone – is that correct?"

"That's right," Simon nodded. "Or by pigeon post if they so wish." He smiled and glanced outside, where a pigeon was strutting on the windowsill, no doubt ready to take orders whenever the librarians wanted to communicate with their customers.

"Leave it with me, then," Vlad said briskly. "If the broadcast goes out now, we'll receive the first replies on Monday morning."

Simon went back to his own office satisfied. Vladimir could be a little difficult on occasion and had disastrous ideas sometimes, but he was dependable. If he said he would do a job, he would do it, and do it by the deadline.

**

Lucy didn't mind Monday mornings; to her, they were just like any other workday morning. She was the first to arrive as usual. She had barely had time to hang her coat on the recently installed coat hook when the phone rang. Picking up the receiver, she noticed that there were three messages on the answerphone.

The call was from a library user whose membership had expired. It was apparently terribly urgent because she had received two emails about it over the weekend, so she was very worried and now fairly pleaded with Lucy for help.

Lucy tucked the receiver under her chin and switched the computer on. Why did she always make the mistake of answering the phone in the morning before she had got the computer running and the system up on the screen? Fortunately the caller was willing to wait. "I'm sorry, there must have been a mistake," Lucy explained, viewing the caller's membership details when she finally had them up on the screen. "According to our database your membership won't expire till next March."

Mimosa entered as Lucy said goodbye to the anxious lady. The phone rang again.

"Oh no!" Lucy let out a wail as soon as she had finished the call. "There is something funny going on with the membership—"

The demanding ringtone tore the air again. This was developing into a nightmare! Mimosa took the call as her computer whirred into action.

"Where is Simon?" Mimosa gasped after the call. "There must be a terrible error somewhere in the system. And where is Vlad?"

"Did I hear somebody mention my name?" the IT librarian asked, peering in. "Why are you two looking so desperate first thing on Monday morning? Surely it can't be so bad working here?"

This was an unusually cheerful greeting from Vladimir, but Mimosa – for once – thought it better not to start arguing with him. She explained the situation quickly while Lucy started checking the answerphone messages. Vlad reminded them that Simon wouldn't come in before lunch because he had a meeting with his line manager.

"Then we'll have to contact a system administrator," Mimosa decided. "Perhaps other TENNIS libraries are experiencing the same problem, or at least the system administrator can log a call with InFamous. I'll ring a few libraries first." InFamous was the company that had provided the regional library management system. The support was normally handled through system administrators, librarians who liaised with InFamous if they couldn't solve a problem themselves.

"Don't worry," Vlad said quickly, "I'll do it. You put the coffee on, we'll need plenty of it today by the look of it."

He disappeared hastily into his office. However, Mimosa had to discard any hopes of making coffee because at that moment Massimo Terremoto came in and was very worried about his expired membership, particularly as he had renewed it only the week before. Of course Mimosa had to deal with Massimo's problem as a matter of urgency, reassuring him that he was still a member of the library and no one was about to take his membership away.

And so the morning went on. Lucy had the brilliant idea of starting a tally of callers so that they would know exactly who had received a message (or two messages, rather) and whether their membership was still valid. Mimosa improved on the idea by suggesting that they should take the opportunity to update the callers' details. This turned out to be very necessary. It was surprising how many people used the library very happily but still forgot to inform library staff that they had moved house, changed their telephone number, or in some cases even their name.

Some callers found the situation quite funny. After all, if you work in a hospital and are told you've expired, then shouldn't the librarians offer you resuscitation? By midday, Mimosa was wishing ardently that she would be offered resuscitation in the form of a cup of strong coffee. She was in no mood for joking. It was a good thing that Vladimir had somehow found the time to make the wonderbrew, and he brought a mug to Mimosa as well as a calming camomile tea to Lucy. I'll never argue with him again, Mimosa thought gratefully; at least not this week.

"It seems that there has been a technical error and the broadcast was sent to all of our readers, and not just once but twice," he commented, warming his hands around the coffee mug.

"What broadcast?" Mimosa asked crossly. "No one told *us* anything about it. We have over a thousand members, so if they all contact us, we'll spend the whole week updating them. I'll give Simon a piece of my mind as soon as he comes in!"

Oh dear, Vladimir thought. He felt sorry for his colleagues who had so abruptly been thrown into this situation. He had offered to tackle the emails that had almost blocked the Healthscare Library's shared inbox, but even so he had only had a fraction of the people that Mimosa and Lucy had had to deal with. Then he shrugged his shoulders and proceeded to write a short news item for the Trust newsletter. "Record number of callers in the library this week," it ran. "Our busy library has experienced a higher volume of business than..." He stopped and changed the phrase to read: "an even higher volume."

Simon returned from his meeting and listened aghast to what his team had to tell him. There were more calls that day and still more on the following day. In fact the whole week seemed to be taken up by the membership affair. The manager could hardly believe his ears when he learned from the system administrator at the end of the week that the IT librarian had chosen the wrong parameters for the broadcast, thus causing the message to be sent to the whole body of Cardigan Bay library members instead of only the expired members – and it had been sent not once but twice during the weekend.

Vladimir listened meekly to what Simon had to say to him, and admitted that the fault was entirely his. Afterwards in his own office, he concluded that it was a small price to pay for the satisfaction of having provided evidence that the library *was* used. Even better, the evidence had come during the annual Enquiries Week when the TENNIS libraries counted all the enquiries they received. What was more, he had escaped suspicion and hadn't been forced to admit to having done it deliberately.

"I bet no other library will score so high this year," he crooned to himself. Eight hundred and forty five enquiries so far, and two more hours to go till the end of Enquiries Week. But he was still sorry for Mimosa and Lucy. Perhaps he would them buy a box of chocolates on Monday.

TWENTY

VLADIMIR'S APPRAISAL

It's a pity one can't access the day except via the morning, Vladimir said to himself as he was getting ready to go to work. Not that he disliked mornings as a rule – it was appraisals he disliked, and he was going to have one first thing that day, at nine o'clock.

Simon's thoughts were running along similar lines as he cycled towards the hospital. Not that he disliked mornings or appraisals – it was the idea of Vladimir's appraisal that he disliked. And why had he chosen to do it first thing that day? To get it over and done with?

The manager and his deputy settled in the former's office with their mugs of coffee and their papers.

"Let's start with what has been good in your work this year," Simon said, shuffling his sheaf of documents and trying to sound brisk even though he was feeling dismally low. A long pause followed, then he drew breath and began. "There is no doubt that your 3D paper stars helped us win the first prize in the Christmas decorating competition. Of course teaching this complicated skill to your colleagues also counts as a training activity."

"Getting Mimosa to produce even a 2D star was something of a feat," was Vladimir's comment. "She is..."

"Never mind Mimosa," the manager interrupted. "We'll come to your relations with her in a minute." He looked at his notes. "Oh yes, you and the others kept the library open and running in January when we had the heavy snowfall. It did not go unnoticed." Neither did your *coup d'état*, he added to himself. "Then there was the episode of the mystery shopper. I was very pleased with your contribution – Victor praised your professional integrity highly."

Professional integrity? Vlad tried to remember what he had said to the mystery shopper, but could only remember what he would have *liked* to say, and that would have landed him on the carpet.

"Your training and search skills are appreciated by customers," Simon went on, speaking rather quickly now. He remembered how he had been taken in by Jill's misunderstanding about the identity of Anastasia. But if a medical secretary could misunderstand a casual remark and think Anastasia was Vlad's pregnant wife, then couldn't Vlad's manager be forgiven for believing the story? Then again, wouldn't any of his illustrious and intelligent librarian ancestors have known better? Simon roused himself. This was no time for ancestor worship. "I liked the way you collaborated with Mimosa on her article. I hear that it's been accepted for publication, with the title *Of Mice and Men: Gender-Related IT Behaviour*," he continued.

"That was easy." Vlad shrugged. "For once she didn't annoy me."

Simon chose to ignore the remark. "However, I'm afraid there are several points where I've heard adverse comments about you or have had reason to criticise you myself," he said.

Vlad's heart sank. Did they really have to discuss his misdemeanours all over again?

"Apparently too much time was spent at the last Junior Doctor induction on how to send an attachment. Now, I know you're an expert on attachments, but really you should be more selective about when to display your expertise."

Vlad pointed out that he always spent half the induction on the subject of attachments anyway, so the last lot of doctors had got exactly the same dose as their predecessors. Simon felt his throat muscles tightening.

"And then, you were heard referring to medical students as—"

"No, I didn't," Vlad protested. "It must have been Mimosa. Or else I called them something else. It doesn't matter now."

Simon sighed. He wanted to say that it mattered a lot, but he suddenly had one of those existential moments where nothing really did seem to matter. He picked up his notes again, fanning himself with the sheaf.

"I was not very happy when you tried to catch a pigeon and even involved Lucy in the scheme," he went on. "There is a Trust policy—"

"Who cares about Trust policies?" Vladimir snorted. "That was an emergency! Don't you remember we had no electricity, no paper, and no pens? I only wanted some quills so we could write by hand, once you'd managed to steal some paper from the photocopying room. Mind you, we didn't have any ink, either, but I'm sure we would have thought of something."

Simon didn't like the word 'steal.' 'Rustling paper' was the term he had used at the time. He decided to ignore the wording. "As to your little *coup d'état* that day when I was snowbound at home, it's best forgotten about," he continued, his facial lines now tensed into Expression 3B. "But the sloppy text message you sent regarding Dr Achinside that led us to believe there was a bomb in the library—"

Vlad jumped up so quickly that a pigeon that had been sunning itself on the window ledge outside flew away in alarm. He reached in his back pocket for his mobile phone to demonstrate how he had arrived at the word 'bomb,' but as Simon didn't want to hear anything more about bombs, Vlad sat down again, cradling the mobile in his hand. He knew there was one more point on Simon's list, and the smoothness of the mobile felt comforting. Rather like a pebble on the beach that had been worn smooth by the waves.

"Last but not least, you recently sent a broadcast to all our readers stating that their library membership had expired, when the message should only have been sent to expired readers, and you somehow managed to send it twice. I do appreciate that this was the first time you'd done a broadcast, and we did discuss the matter afterwards (as befits reflective practice), but I can't help thinking... perhaps you hadn't taken in the instructions with your usual care," Simon said with deliberation. He had always had a suspicion that there was more to the story, but it was hard to believe that Vlad would have acted on purpose.

"Well, it's time we discussed your Personal Development Plan," the manager said when Vlad remained silent. "First of all, what's that new product you said you'd like to work on?"

The IT librarian leaned forward, his blue eyes now full of passion. "It's FROSTBITE, which stands for a FRequency Operated STandard Barcodable IT Experience. It will solve all our interlibrary service problems! But I need three or four hours dedicated time per week to develop it."

Simon felt relieved. This sounded much more reasonable than what he had feared, and he promised to discuss the arrangements at the next team meeting. But there was still that personal development goal from the previous year that Vlad had not yet achieved: learning to smile. He had never been known to smile, and customers sometimes commented on his dour looks. Wasn't smiling supposed to be something natural, Simon wondered; one of the human universals, or whatever they were called?

"Now come on, Vlad, you really must learn to smile," he coaxed. "Five minutes every day in front of the mirror. Open your mouth as if you were in the dentist's chair, but only stretch it sideways, then... then pull your cheeks upwards. No, not with your hands, just use your cheek muscles. We'll hang a mirror in the staff room so you can practise during your lunch break. Perhaps Mimosa - well, no, perhaps Lucy can coach you." He tried to sound encouraging, but in his heart he knew Vladimir would fail once again.

TWENTY-ONE

MIMOSA'S TEMPTATION

Mimosa was called into Simon's office one day and given a lecture on why she should keep an eye on her annual leave allowance, which up till now she had used so sparingly that it made the library manager look like a slave driver. Mimosa tried to explain that she had too much to do to think about annual leave, but Simon classified that excuse under Never-Ending Expenditure of Time and said (promised? threatened?) that they would discuss the matter later. He made a note for himself to consult a book called *In Search of Lost Time*, which he had heard of recently; it must be a very thorough study as it apparently ran into thirteen volumes. He could always start with an executive summary if one was available.

So now Mimosa was sulking in her office. In other workplaces people were criticised for not working hard enough, but here it was the opposite. Very well then, she would use all her annual leave, whether or not she got all her jobs done. Simon would have to pick up the pieces himself. That would be real evidence-based time management.

This thought gave her a little satisfaction. She turned to the most hated task of the week, which was answering the queries that had been posted on CARBuncle, their new enquiry service. They all took turns to look after it, but Mimosa was the only one who didn't like doing it.

"Hi CARBuncle," the first query ran. "Where can I get hold of the hypocratic oath?"

Mimosa sighed. She wanted to reply: "If you knew how to spell the name of the Father of Medicine, you would find the answer easily" or something to that effect. But Simon wouldn't like it if he saw such a rude reply, and anyway, rudeness was more in Vladimir's line – she didn't want to act out of character. She therefore pressed the reply button and started typing: "You mean the Hippocratic Oath..." In any case, googling would probably have automatically suggested the correct spelling, but Mimosa didn't want to promote searching the internet if she could possibly avoid it. They had enough trouble persuading people to use clinical databases for information on clinical topics.

Lucy came in and flung herself in her chair. "Simon has just given me a telling off because I'm too conscientious," she told her colleague, her voice trembling. "He said I always check our—"

Mimosa interrupted her. "I know. He doesn't want us to wear ourselves out, he says. But it's this stupid CARBuncle that wears *me* out."

At that point, Vladimir sauntered in and turned to the assistant librarian. "Good job you're into CARBuncle just now, Samosa. Somebody phoned and wanted to know about human gibbons. I said ask CARBuncle, I've no idea what human gibbons are," he said, pushing his hands in his pockets.

Mimosa was furious. "Gibbon yourself, it's human *givens* they're talking about. And if you call me Samosa again, I'll take out a grievance against you for bullying," she snapped and turned to her PC again. Why did she have to work in a place like this? Even in this age of austerity, there must be places that could employ a chartered, experienced, hard-working librarian and show her a bit of appreciation.

As soon as Vlad had gone back into his office, she logged out of CARBuncle and on to the librarians' professional website, then clicked on Jobs and Careers. She would find a new job somewhere really nice, in a library full of pleasant and intelligent colleagues. Maybe in another part of the country altogether?

Her dream job was staring at her from the screen. A deputy manager's post at Eventide College of Cataloguing, reporting to the senior library manager, Mr Furber. Or that's what they must have meant – 'senile library manager' was clearly just an embarrassing typo. Mimosa was sure this must be the Furber that the speaker had constantly referred to at the catalogue development event she had attended recently. Who else could it be? Fred Furber himself!

**

And so it happened that a few weeks later, Mimosa was standing at the door of the Eventide College of Cataloguing. It had taken her a while to find the door among the ivy that covered the building, but here she was, ready for her job interview for the deputy manager's post.

The place smelled romantically musty compared to the recently refurbished Cardigan Bay Healthscare Library. Paint smell was so, so... clinical. Chemical. This was much nicer. The floorboards creaked rhythmically and encouragingly all the way through the maze that took her to the interviewing room, which must have been the old assembly hall of the college. It didn't matter that the hall was as cold as the grave, Mimosa's circulation was working overtime with excitement.

It was a pity of course that Mr Furber turned out to be an ordinary library manager and no one famous. But perhaps the library would become famous one day, what with the innovations that the reinforced team would bring about. Not that there was any money, but... Yes, money was a problem. Her starting salary would be so small that it would barely cover her bus fares to and from that nice little house she had spotted on the other side of the town, but she could always cycle to work and become fabulously fit. Since the college kitchen had been closed down due to another case of food poisoning, she would have to bring her own sandwiches, but she didn't mind; it would work out cheaper and save some more money.

After the interview, Mimosa was shown round by the library sub-assistant, who scuttled so quickly between the shelves that Mimosa could hardly keep up with him. In a shady corner of the echoing reading room – they really had to keep their voices down – he stopped and pulled out a rather worn book, clearly with some pride. Mimosa picked it up gingerly, afraid to touch it in case it crumbled.

"It's all right," the sub-assistant assured her. "It won't fall to pieces just yet. But you'll want to wash your hands afterwards in case the mice have, you know... defecated on it. Though I shouldn't have thought so, they seem to prefer nibbling at it. But it's a great book, that. It's the third edition and our readers are still using it even though I hear it's now reached the tenth edition, or was it eleventh?"

The sub-assistant looked at Mimosa expectantly. "We've got loads more like this, you'll see them all if you start working here. I hope you will, and I hope you'll stay, too. I'm fed up with having a new deputy manager every month. The previous one left only after a week, as a matter of fact," he explained, shoving the mouse-eaten volume back into its dusty corner. "We've recently had another new colleague," he continued. "We used to have a senior library assistant called Abe. He had worked over sixty years at Eventide College, but then he was finally got rid of when Human Resources noticed he was still around. He had a leaving party with a cake which had real candles on it. But his nylon shirt sleeve caught the flame and melted, and the cleaner who had made the cake and put candles on it was dismissed. So, then we had to replace both the cleaner and Abe. That was a pity because Jed always kept the oil lamps so clean. As a matter of fact, the college couldn't afford to replace him, so now we take turns cleaning the library ourselves."

He opened the door that led back into the corridor. "You'd better go now if you want to catch the train," he warned Mimosa. "There's just the one service a day."

***

Mimosa returned to her own library the following day. She had told no one why she had taken the day off, not even Lucy. The first person she saw in the familiar hospital corridor was Brendan Brill, Senior Occupational Therapist. He greeted her cheerfully and promised to come in soon to discuss new book titles. "There is a new edition of one of our key texts, and I'd like you to purchase it for the library if possible," he said.

New editions... Mimosa's heart beat faster as she climbed the stairs to the library, and it wasn't because she was not fit. She opened the door and thought she could distinguish a faint paint smell still lingering from the time of the refurbishment, but perhaps it was just Adonis' cleaning products. But the smell of coffee was unmistakeable. Oh, it was good to be back!

She opened the door of the staff room. There was Vladimir, pouring coffee into two mugs. "Hi, Sam—Mimosa," he said. "I'm just doing our coffees, shall I pour one for you as well?"

Mimosa stepped forward and flung her arms round her astounded colleague.

TWENTY-TWO

A BODY IN THE LIBRARY

Mimosa switched on her PC. While it was going through its check-ups, she started her own check-ups – the library's morning routines – because Lucy had a dental appointment and would come in late.

Everything was all right in the photocopying area. That was suspicious. How come no one had been in the library out of hours to print off articles or flight tickets or car advertisements? Most mornings, copies of forgotten documents (or parts thereof) were found lying around the multifunction device. Ominous, Mimosa said to herself. A sure sign that the machine was jammed or out of paper or out of toner, or simply broken. Just her luck to have to deal with it.

She examined the MFD (which Vladimir had once said must be short for 'Much Fuss, Dammit!') but found nothing wrong with it. She opened each tray in turn to replenish the paper. Almost untouched: perhaps there had been no overnight users, then.

She continued her tour into the reading room. Opening the door, she immediately saw the open window and felt the cold air. So, somebody *had* been in and had forgotten to shut the window. Why couldn't people close a window that they had opened? Why couldn't they treat the library a bit more like their own homes?

Mimosa paused on the threshold and smiled wryly. Treating the library like their own homes might mean even more empty Coke bottles and biscuit crumbs. But leaving a window open was a matter of Health and Safety. She had often expressed this view to Simon and had asked for permission to put up a strongly worded reminder or – better still – to send an email to all users, but every time he had said no, in a very managerial tone of voice. "We don't want to scare them away, we want them to use the library more. Besides, you've got better things to do than send reminders to people. What about those new books that want cataloguing?"

Mimosa walked round the big table in the bay to close the window. This time, she would find out from Reception who had signed out the key to access the library overnight, but she wouldn't tell Simon that she had asked. This time she—

That was when she saw the head. A grey head with a red-rimmed eye, dangling limply from the windowsill. And a spot of blood nearby.

Nothing in Mimosa's library studies had prepared her for this. Nothing whatsoever had been offered by the Library Science department, not even a random joke about a body in the library. Neither had her training in the Trust prepared her, except possibly the fire awareness training, in which they had been told not to panic. "Pause for a moment before taking action," she whispered to herself, trying not to look at the grey head. But what action should she take?

A horrible thought crossed her mind. What if Lucy, who was so sensitive, came in before the body had been removed? Mimosa tried to think clearly, but the grey head and red-rimmed eye came back to her although she was looking the other way. If only Simon was here, or even Vladimir – but not a reader. A reader would expect her to act professionally and coolly, whereas her colleagues would share the problem. With any luck, they wouldn't even notice that she was trembling.

How had the body got there? The window was wide open. Mimosa felt a surge of bitterness. This time she *would* get the reader who had forgotten to close the window. Never mind what Simon said, she would not let the matter rest. The thought sent the adrenaline flowing, and she marched out of the reading room, closed the door behind her and rolled a chair in front of it to deter people from entering.

Just then the front door opened. It was Vladimir. What if he laughs at me when he notices I'm upset? Mimosa thought. He stopped when he saw her standing stock still in the middle of the lobby. He also noticed the chair that was blocking the entrance to the reading room. Something was afoot.

"Vlad," Mimosa started. "There's something in the reading room." She paused. Her head was beginning to throb. But she was determined she would not start crying – not in front of Vlad.

"Yes?" he said encouragingly. This was clearly not the right moment to start teasing Mimosa, though he was tempted to do so: of course there was always *something* in the reading room. Also, he remembered he hadn't called her Samosa for a long time, which never failed to annoy her. Not now, he thought; I'll save it till later.

Mimosa collected herself. She would sound as calm and composed as a whole conference of senior librarians. "There's a body in the reading room," she announced, turned on her heels, pushed the chair away and entered. The grey head and red eye were still there (of course they were!) and she felt queasy.

"Oh dear," Vlad said, stopping in his tracks. "We'd better call Adonis. How did it happen?"

"The blighters must have left the window open again," Mimosa said. "But this time I'm going to get them."

"The Estates manager says we should have pigeon chains on the windows," Vlad said. "Looks like he's right. I reckon the poor thing hit the window when it was open on a crack, then crawled inside to die."

Mimosa shuddered. The cleaner... of course, that was the sensible thing to do. But she wanted a photo of the body as evidence even though she didn't feel like looking at the dead bird. Could she ask Vlad to take it?

"We'd better be careful how we tell Lucy about this," Vlad said. "She's so sensitive. I'm sure she couldn't have coped as well as you. Why don't you go and put the coffee on, and I'll ring Adonis? Oh, and I'll take a picture of this on my mobile. It's time we taught those careless customers a lesson. We'll publish the picture in the Trust newsletter and call it: *A body in the library.*"

***

Simon was on his way to the library. He turned the corner just in time to see Adonis coming out. The cleaner was carrying a bundle in his hand with something grey sticking out of it, and the look of disgust on his face confirmed Simon's suspicion: the bundle contained a dead pigeon.

Simon's field of vision was filled with a flash of red so strong that it erased the grey of the dead bird completely. This time he would get Vladimir... Why had he wanted a pigeon *now*? There was no need for quills – not a real nor an imaginary need, unlike that day when they'd run out of pens and the printer had ceased to function.

This must be what having high blood pressure is like, Simon thought, feeling he could suffocate with rage. Perhaps his blood pressure *was* high right now. He wrenched the library door open and wished it had come off its hinges. He stormed into the staff room, from which a smell of coffee was emanating, and heard two familiar voices for once not arguing with each other.

Before Simon could open his mouth, Vlad turned to him and spoke. "We've had a spot of bother here this morning, Simon," he announced, taking another mug from the shelf and filling it for his manager. "Mimosa found a dead pigeon on the reading room windowsill. Adonis has just removed it."

"And how did the pigeon get there?" Simon demanded to know, still belligerent. Then he repented. They both looked so serious, yet in agreement with each other. If Vlad had killed the bird, there would have been a full scale battle going on.

"We don't know," Mimosa said. "It was there when I came in." She proceeded to tell the story, and her voice only shook once.

"Old Moore-Gubbins was right, then," Simon sighed. "We must have chains in the windows. Mimosa, can you fill in a New Works request to that effect and fax it to Estates?"

"A chained library," she said dreamily. "That's what they used to have in the seventeenth century, or whenever it was.

I've always wanted that, but only for the books and not for keeping pigeons out."

"Chained readers," Vladimir suggested, baring his teeth. "Not chained books. We could—"

Simon interrupted him. "No, we couldn't," he said firmly. "Back to work, both of you!"

TWENTY-THREE

THE CONSTANT GARDENER

The reading room of the Healthscare Library was nice and sunny, with large windows and wide windowsills. There were a couple of easy chairs and a comfortable sofa as well as two three computer workstations and a large old table and chairs – the founder's dining room suite – and of course bookshelves arranged to best effect and a handsome display unit for new titles. The windowsills were often graced with flowering plants that had been donated by grateful library users. But now there were none left and the place looked a little sad in spite of having been refurbished so thoroughly. Only a pale spider plant stood on top of a shelf gathering cobwebs.

Simon suggested that they ought to grow something themselves because plants were good for the image of the library; users often commented on how welcoming the place looked with them. Both Lucy and Mimosa were half-hearted about the idea though.

"It will take too much time," they said. "But of course *you* can do it if you like." Simon's reply was that he wasn't much good at house plants, and besides, he had too much to do already. However, he was quite sure he was right and told Mimosa to do a literature search on the effect of plants – especially flowering plants – on library users. "How plants enhance the library experience," he specified with a solemn tone of voice. But the results of the literature search were not entirely satisfactory. Apparently there was very little reliable evidence as yet, and since none of the CARB team seemed to be willing to look after new plants, it was even more unlikely they would wish to set up a study to provide the evidence themselves.

Vladimir didn't say anything, but he was listening to the conversation. A few days later, he appeared with two strange-looking plants and placed them on the reading room windowsill, where flies were buzzing in the sunshine and annoying the readers.

"Venus flytraps," he explained triumphantly to his puzzled colleagues. "They'll make the place look more cheerful, and we'll get rid of the flies. Killing two flies with one stone, as you might say."

"Yes, as *you* might say," was Mimosa's dry comment. She was not impressed. What was cheerful about Venus flytraps? But she didn't feel like arguing with Vlad, since he had taken a step towards providing that enhanced library experience. She on her part would be quite happy to provide new books and other forms of information for their customers.

All was well and the flytraps enjoyed their diet, until Adonis squirted insect killer on the flies and also accidentally on the plants and on a few readers. The nourishing flies were no more, the most sensitive of the readers made a complaint, and the plants began to wilt.

But Vladimir did not give up. He next produced a seed tray and was seen tending it every day in the reading room until Simon found the packet that had contained the seeds. He called Vlad into his office.

"You can't do this," the manager barked. "We'll be arrested for growing illegal drugs!"

"But it's only hemp to provide fibres. I've always felt sorry I destroyed the curtains when we were trying to have the library refurbished, so I thought..." Vlad began to defend his choice.

"Never mind the curtains, we've got new ones now! You can't be serious," Simon retorted. "Get rid of that tray at once!"

"But you said we should grow something ourselves," Vlad reminded him. "You didn't say it had to be something traditional, like geraniums or..."

Simon refused to hear any more, but marched into the reading room and tipped the contents of the tray into the bin. Vlad returned to his office and sulked for the rest of the week.

The next project involved two enormous growbags. They didn't fit on the windowsill properly, and Adonis complained to Simon because of the extra cleaning he had had to do after one of the bags fell on the floor and spilled its contents.

"What on earth are those bags for, Vlad?" Simon demanded to know.

"Earth," was the curt answer. After some questioning, Simon found out that they were intended for cherry tomatoes, which Vlad had raised at home and was about to bring in for transplanting. The men decided to compromise: Vlad would be allowed to plant his tomatoes, but into large pots and not into growbags.

And so it came about that the reading room at Cardigan Bay had twenty tomato plants on the windowsills. As the summer wore on, the plants grew taller and spread vigorously until they covered the windows, making the reading room quite shady. A sensitive customer complained because the tomato smell was overpowering and the humidity had risen noticeably, but by that time even Simon was on the gardener's side and wouldn't listen to complaints. "As long as they don't go and tell Claire that we're spending working time tending to plants," he commented to his team. Lucy suggested they could send a punnet of tomatoes to Claire, but Simon was horrified at the idea, and Lucy spent the rest of the day feeling guilty.

Vlad in his turn lodged a complaint because some thoughtless readers had used plant pots for hiding their sandwich wrappers in; this had tempted a pigeon to try to squeeze in under the pigeon chains in search of crumbs. It had got stuck (after all, the chains were meant to deter pigeons and had been carefully measured for size) and had to be rescued by Vlad, who received a couple of furious pecks on his fingers in the process. "You ought to be glad the pigeon wasn't seriously injured," Mimosa said. "I mean, if it was vigorous enough to peck you?" Vlad muttered something like, "What about *my* injuries, then?" But Mimosa had already turned to answer the phone.

One morning, Mimosa and Lucy were chatting idly in Simon's absence and forgetting all about work, when Vlad came in with a bundle of long bamboo canes under his arm.

"What are those for?" Lucy asked with idle curiosity, leaning on the office doorframe.

"Staff management," was the brief reply. Lucy scuttled back to her desk, started typing frantically and didn't stop until lunchbreak. Meanwhile, Vlad propped up the wobbly tomato plants with the canes.

When the tomatoes began to ripen towards the end of the summer, they were sampled daily by the library staff – Vlad suspected that a few readers also sampled them – and a Tomatofest was being planned to attract new library users. Simon seemed to have forgotten all about keeping his line manager in the dark about their gardening activities. But before they got as far as announcing the Tomatofest, the Trust provided them with another idea.

"Staff wellbeing competition," Simon read out from the Trust newsletter one day. "The winning department must produce an original idea to promote staff health and wellbeing."

"I think I know which department is going to win that competition," Lucy smiled.

And she was right.

TWENTY-FOUR

WHAT LUCY DID

Lucy glanced at her watch again and hurried her steps. She had forgotten to put up a notice to say that the Healthscare Library would not be staffed that day due to a teambuilding exercise, so now she had to do it before Simon picked her up in his car from the main entrance of the hospital.

The Trust management had announced that all teams and departments had to have a teambuilding day. Simon had welcomed the idea and had selected the option of helping an elderly lady with gardening, as that seemed a safer and more constructive option than gokarting or abseiling, which were among the suggestions put forward by the Trust. Besides, Vladimir had shown an interest in gardening, so it was likely that he would cooperate (something that could never be taken for granted).

No customers were in sight as Lucy entered the library. That was a good thing – she didn't want to have to answer queries and solve problems now, and sometimes saying 'no' took as long as doing the thing which was requested. "Just this once..." "It won't take a minute..." Lucy could imagine the pleading tone of voice only too well.

She unlocked the door of the office and picked up an envelope that had been posted under the door. Probably photocopying money from a user who had failed to pay but had now had a pang of conscience. Lucy slipped the envelope into the desk drawer where the cash tin was kept and locked it again. The bookkeeping would have to wait until the following day. She collected the sticky tape and the notice, which was ready waiting on her desk, and slipped out. She was positioning the notice carefully on the outside of the front door when a young visiting researcher approached her.

"I wonder if you could help me," she said in her best English, sounding slightly apologetic. "I have an eye infection, but my housemates don't know how to put these drops in my eyes, and I've never done it myself."

Lucy decided it was best to help the researcher rather than go in search of somebody with more experience. She asked the researcher to sit down in the office while she read the instructions, washed her hands and administered the drops, explaining carefully how the researcher should do it herself in the evening.

The things we're asked to do, Lucy said to herself after the researcher had left. The phone rang, and she thought it best to answer in case it was something to do with the teambuilding day. It was the wrong number, but the lady at the other end was adamant that this *was* the number for Mr So-and-so, Slouch Ward. Lucy wondered whether it was a patient or a doctor that the lady was trying to get hold of; putting her through to the switchboard apparently wasn't acceptable, but that was what she had to do in the end, explaining to the lady kindly but firmly that it was the best option.

Time was running out, and she hadn't dealt with her notice yet. Simon would be waiting already. Lucy felt that being late was not a good start for a teambuilding day. But she had had no choice: she had helped two people with urgent needs; in passing, she had also replenished the photocopier tray with paper, shredded a confidential document that had been left lying around, deposited the photocopying money safely in her desk drawer... and now she could finally stick that notice on the door.

She dropped the sticky tape, and it came out of its holder and rolled under the returned books trolley. Since the massive trolley was on casters, it wasn't too difficult to manoeuvre it. It was sheer bad luck that she had to push it temporarily in front of the ladies' toilet door and there was somebody in there who wanted to come out at that precise moment. Lucy chose to ignore the banging on the door for those two minutes that she needed to find the roll and return the trolley to its original position. Explaining to the trapped lady what had happened was also a quick matter, except that the lady then wanted to know how to join the library. Lucy stifled a sigh, ran in to pick up a registration form and promised to be back the following day to show the new user around.

At last the notice was in place and the sticky tape back on Lucy's desk. She slammed the office door shut but had a fleeting thought that she might just have forgotten to take her keys with her – but no, they were safely in her handbag. She hesitated for one more moment, looking round the lobby as if for the last time; who knows, they might find the library gone when they returned the following day, as it had done that time when they'd been relocated so traumatically. But no, she must not keep her colleagues waiting. Hurrying through the lobby, she cast a disapproving glance at a chocolate wrapper that was lying under a computer workstation, which she hadn't noticed before. She opened the front door, and in came Ben, one of their more eccentric users. She let him pass, determined not to get involved in any conversations.

But Ben had a different idea.

"Hi, Lucy," he greeted her cheerfully. "How d'you like this?" Turning his back to her, he swiftly yanked down his jogging pants to reveal an elaborate flower tattoo which decorated the upper part of his rear.

Fortunately, saying "very nice" is something one can utter almost on autopilot, and that was exactly what Lucy did. Then she escaped into the corridor. Ben, evidently satisfied with her response, disappeared into the reading room.

Half way down the corridor, the flustered Lucy met Simon, who had got tired of waiting in his car and had come upstairs to see what was holding her up.

"Simon, you'll never believe what Ben did," Lucy started, forgetting to apologise for being late. "He showed me his... his..." She hesitated, searching for a polite word.

Simon turned to stare at her in disbelief. "You mean his... no—o, surely not?!"

"His flower tattoo," Lucy explained, slightly out of breath as she was trotting down the stairs and trying to keep up with Simon.

The library manager shook his head. A flower tattoo? What was so shocking about that? Really, Lucy was a bit too sensitive sometimes.

TWENTY-FIVE

VLADIMIR LEARNS TO SMILE

Simon and Lucy hurried to the car, where Mimosa and Vladimir were already sitting and practising a mutual sulk. Oh dear, Simon thought, the mandatory teambuilding day hasn't started very well. He comforted himself with the thought that other departments probably fared just as badly, though he hadn't heard anything from managers who had already had theirs.

The reasons for the sulking were as follows. First of all, as they were arranging their seating in Simon's car before driving off to pick up Lucy, Mimosa noticed the fire engine red T-shirt that Vladimir was wearing, and commented on what a good warning colour it was. That in itself wasn't a very offensive remark, but coming from Mimosa and aimed at Vlad, one could be sure it was meant to be, and that of course was how he took it. Simon therefore quickly intervened by telling Mimosa off sharply, which then put her in a bad mood.

The other reason for the mutual sulk had begun to develop the day before. Mimosa had seen Vlad sitting in his office looking extremely serious if not downright ill, yet apparently concentrating very hard. Only his ears moved slowly. Mimosa had exclaimed in horror and asked after his health.

Vlad had found it too embarrassing to explain that he was practising smiling because it was one of his Professional Development Goals; instead, he told her that he was practising mindfulness meditation – the first thing that sprung to his mind. And now, while they were sitting in the car and waiting for the others, Mimosa had started to question him about it. The result had been disastrous, and certainly not conducive to Vlad learning how to smile.

Fifty-fifty, Simon said to himself. Two sulking, two not sulking. Better look at things positively. He started the car after making sure that they were all securely in their seats and sped down the hospital drive in a manner that would have done credit to any rally driver. Lucy glanced shyly at her colleagues. They all looked so different from their everyday selves, wearing T-shirts with text and pictures – normally forbidden by the Trust dress code – and faded jeans. She was wearing Bermuda shorts as she was hoping the day would be warm.

The library team had chosen to help Granny (as the old lady was generally known), a former patient who was now being rehabilitated back into her own home. Simon didn't have a satnav in his ancient car, and they quarrelled terribly as they drove to Granny's house, disagreeing at every possible crossroads and roundabout. This method was relatively successful as they only lost their way three times and arrived conveniently at lunch time. A soup lunch quickly produced by Granny and Lucy while the others argued about laying the table and who would help with the washing up. Afterwards, they finally got down to some gardening. Granny told them what jobs needed doing, and the team brought out the tools from the shed; the division of labour was achieved simply by everyone grabbing whatever tool they could first lay their hands on.

Lucy decided to take the big shears and tidy up a straggly bush before anyone else volunteered for the job. It looked like something light and artistic, although she had never tried it before. But there was always a first time, and it was good to practise a new skill. Simon would be pleased with her.

The team dispersed into various parts of the large garden, and Lucy quite forgot about her colleagues' existence. The sun was shining pleasantly – not too hot, not too bright – and she felt happy and relaxed for the first time that day. After half an hour's clipping and snipping, she laid down the shears. She hadn't realised how heavy they were. She had a look at her handiwork, walking round the bush and rubbing her slender arms and wrists to ease the muscles that had begun to ache. She might snip another bit off here and there, but generally it was not bad for a first attempt... Ow! Something sharp and heavy hit her bare leg. She had forgotten about the shears and had tripped over them. She sat down on the grass and examined her leg. It was bleeding.

Simon stood at the kitchen door watching his team at work. A very satisfying sight, that. He himself had finished his task in record time. Granny had disappeared into the lounge to arrange the tea things because she insisted they should have their afternoon tea there, and Mimosa had actually volunteered to give her a hand. Everything was calm, and Simon was beginning to enjoy his day at last. A teambuilding day was not a day off for a manager, but he could be forgiven for letting his hair down for a minute or two.

Suddenly he saw how Lucy sat down, evidently in distress. Then Vladimir ran across the lawn and up to the house, rushed into the kitchen pushing Simon aside, and out again with one of Granny's tea towels before anyone had time to ask what the matter was. Mimosa came out of the lounge with an empty tray and peered from behind Simon's shoulder, and together they watched Vlad, who was kneeling in the grass and bandaging Lucy's leg.

It seemed to take a very long time, and Simon was becoming worried. Vlad was still on his knees, and an incredible thought struck both Simon and Mimosa at the same time. Could it be...?

Just then Vlad finally stood up and walked up to the house. His face was twisted into a strange shape, such as they had never seen before.

"What's the matter with him?" Mimosa whispered anxiously.

"He's smiling," Simon whispered back, as Vlad stepped up to where they were standing.

"Simon, I don't think Lucy and I will need to do any more teambuilding," Vlad announced solemnly, but still smiling.

They had guessed right, then. The library manager smiled broadly in return and extended his hand to the younger man to congratulate him, but Vlad felt he owed the others an explanation. "I thought as I was on my knees anyway, I might as well pop the question," he said, and his smile changed into a grin.

Mimosa realised she had been holding her breath and also grabbing Simon's arm, which she now let go. Apparently

Simon hadn't noticed anything, for his whole attention was directed towards Vlad.

"You're wrong about the teambuilding, Vlad," he said. "This is just where it begins."

TWENTY-SIX

WATCH OUT, TEAM!

They were all very quiet on the way back from Granny's. Vladimir and Lucy sat in the back. I bet they're holding hands, Mimosa thought, but didn't want to turn round to look. Vlad was sitting behind her, and every now and then he shifted himself to make his long legs more comfortable, which only resulted in him banging them against Mimosa's seat. It irritated her. She should have asked Simon to stop so she could have adjusted the seat to give Vlad more room, but she didn't feel like it. She would have to make enough adjustments later on, now that those two were engaged. What did Lucy see in Vlad, anyway? It was she, Mimosa, who had always argued with him – she had taken notice of him and he of her, even if they'd never had a kind word to say to each other. Oh well, that wasn't quite true; they had managed to put together a publishable article without quarrelling. But now – would she be able to argue with Vlad in front of Lucy?

And why had neither Lucy nor Vladimir ever dropped the slightest hint to the others? Had they really only seen each other in a new light today?

Simon was hoping the others would think he was concentrating on driving, but in reality his silence was due to the fact that he was worried. Now that half his team was engaged to each other, the logical conclusion was that they would take their annual leave at the same time in the future. It had of course happened occasionally before by coincidence, but the team had always tried to avoid such coincidences. Simon thought of other libraries he knew. What was the composition of their staff like? If he could think of any other couples, maybe he could approach their manager discreetly and enquire how things were run elsewhere. Perhaps he could do a literature search and see if anything had been written on this topic. Simon grinned to himself: evidence based staff management. That's what he wanted.

Mimosa tried to feel sorry for Lucy because of her injured leg, but couldn't quite. Perhaps the wound was so bad that Lucy wouldn't be able to work tomorrow? In that case Mimosa would have to take care of all the medical student registrations they'd been working on. That made at least a dozen on top of her own workload, unless Lucy had completed her batch, which she couldn't possibly have done. Not even Lucy, who was almost perfect, but not quite – only intermittently.

Lucy seemed happy enough without Mimosa's sympathy. Her leg hurt, but not very much. She glanced at Vlad, who was holding her hand. She wanted to say something to him, but felt too shy in their colleagues' presence. Why was everybody so quiet? They couldn't be terribly tired after that amount of physical exercise, even though they weren't exactly athletic any of them. If only somebody would say something... Were they cross with her?

Vladimir was getting fed up with his cramped position in the back seat. Mimosa should have had more sense before they set off, and offered to shift her seat forward. But then when had she ever shown any consideration for him and his wishes or his ideas? All right, true, they had managed to write that article on gender based IT behaviour without arguing. Even Simon had noticed that and had been pleased. But the credit wasn't all due to Mimosa; he, Vlad, had shown remarkable self-restraint in not once calling her Samosa or doing any of the other things that usually annoyed Ms MacAroon so unduly.

The silence was broken violently by Mimosa's agitated cry. "Simon, watch out!"

The driver stood on the brakes instinctively. They had nearly missed a turning that looked familiar to Simon, but apart from that, he couldn't see any danger that they had narrowly avoided. He turned to Mimosa, baring his teeth in his rage. "What do you mean, watch out? Where's the danger? You should know better than scream like that, you're a driver yourself and should know that a—"

"It's that idiot, Samosa, don't take any notice of her," Vlad snorted, rubbing his knees, which he had hit on the back of the front seat.

"Of course I called out! It's only natural that somebody should keep their eyes open in this place. We had enough trouble getting there in the morning, and we were already late setting off, thanks to our perfectionist—" Mimosa didn't have time to finish her sentence, because Lucy raised her voice.

"We wouldn't have had any trouble getting here, if Mister Library Manager had had a satnav in his rusty old crate. Who wants to—"

Simon gasped. No one had ever heard Lucy talk like that. All right, they were not in the library exactly, but by Jove, this was still a working day, and the others, including the library assistant, should show due respect to him. So before Lucy had finished her sentence, Simon bawled out a reply.

And so all was as before with the CARB team. They continued there by the roadside for half an hour, everyone accusing each other and raising their voices. Simon with his well-trained baritone was particularly good at drowning everybody else's comments, but Lucy had the advantage of a voice that could rise up the scale to glass-breaking heights.

In the end, the small car was so filled with the din that Mimosa had to wind down the window on her side. That was when she noticed the police car. It was approaching fast behind them. Then it stopped, and a policewoman got out and walked briskly to the oddly parked car. As soon as she was convinced that the four people inside were all right in spite of their clearly agitated state, she proceeded to issue a ticket to the driver because he had parked in a dangerous place near a major crossroads.

"Who's going to pay this fine?" Simon grumbled after the officer had left. "It's all due to this damned team building day that we got it."

"*You* got it," Mimosa corrected him coldly.

"But it was you who told Simon to stop," Lucy reminded her, indignant that Mimosa should have forgotten her share in the events.

"Now, let's on no account start again..." The library manager sighed. "Never mind, talking of accounts, perhaps I can pass it on to Claire as expenses."

The thought of Claire Twinsett having to pay expenses – especially of this type – so cheered everyone that they all chuckled. Everything felt suddenly in place again. Simon turned the car in the right direction and raised his voice once again, this time to sing snatches of a piece that his choir was going to perform the following week, and that kept the others quiet the rest of the way back home. The team had narrowly survived the teambuilding day in one piece; they could afford to be magnanimous towards their manager, who after all did have quite a good voice.

TWENTY-SEVEN

BEWARE OF THE LIBRARY ASSISTANT

Mimosa looked up from her work when a nursing student approached Lucy's desk, speaking in a whisper. Their customers didn't usually whisper, so what was the matter? Had the girl lost her voice?

"I think Hector's taken out a reference book," the girl said. "In fact I'm sure he has. We heard him say he was going to do so at the weekend, and the book isn't there now. But mind you, don't tell him I told you!" With that, she turned and left.

Lucy sighed and got up to do a shelf check. Yes, Dora was unfortunately right. Their only copy, a reference copy, of *Principles of Theoretical Nursing Practice* had disappeared from the reference collection. Lucy searched the nearby shelves and then the nursing section of the loan collection, but the book simply wasn't there.

She reported this to Mimosa.

"All right, we'll mark it as *Missing* on the catalogue, but I'm not going to buy a replacement copy in a hurry if it's true that Hector has taken the book for a walk. It's very expensive. We'd better wait and see," Mimosa reflected. As an interim measure, she emailed the aggrieved student explaining how to access the book on My Little e-Library – sorry,

Eeksperience (as the NHS electronic library was now called) – and sent a cautiously worded email to Hector.

"I'm fed up with students," Lucy moaned in the staff room. "They're all over the place, they don't always even know whether they're seconded or on placement, they steal our books..."

Simon admonished her gently. "It's not as bad as all that, you know. That's only two or three students we're talking about. Of course Hector will deny he's taken out a reference copy – who wouldn't? I'm sure it will come back after he's finished this module in his studies. These things happen in all libraries, not just ours."

The library manager returned to his office and found a student sitting in his chair, about to log out of Simon's email account. "This was the only free computer," the lad explained, ducking slightly under Simon's murderous glance.

But Lucy was not content to let matters lie. She had been battling valiantly to provide a good service in spite of her workload (the teambuilding day had only made matters worse because they had in effect lost one working day), and not only had she served the swarming students, but countless other users as well. She and Mimosa had recently completed a stock take, which had shown several items to be missing, including copies of nursing textbooks and junior doctors' exam fodder. No wonder Lucy looked ready to be floored – or to take action.

She waited until she knew Simon would be away for a few days. Then she approached Vladimir as he was the only one besides Simon who was authorised to send announcements to the Trust intranet on behalf of the Library Services.

"Vlad, I've got an urgent message to put on the intranet. Please can you do it for me?" she asked with glowing cheeks, a piece of paper in her hand.

"All right, let's see it then," her fiancé said, examining the paper. The announcement read as follows:

To all Trust staff and students: A reference copy of a nursing textbook has been accidentally removed from the Healthscare Library. As it is contaminated and therefore poses a severe health risk, please return it to the library ASAP."

"You'll never get away with this, Lu," he said seriously. "Simon will flay you and Infection Control will investigate the matter. You've not even said what the contamination is, though perhaps it's just as well since it might not sound plausible." But deep down, Vlad was pleased that Lucy had shown such determination, so he placed the announcement on the intranet. Then they sat back and waited for results.

***

The following morning, Hector was seen skulking around the book returns trolley in the corridor with a scarf tied round his nose and mouth. After he had gone, Lucy went to check the trolley, and there was the missing *Principles* wrapped in a bright yellow plastic bag. She carried it in triumphantly.

"Well done, Lucy," Mimosa said admiringly. "I wouldn't have believed it of you!" She turned to her computer, looked up the book in the catalogue and changed its status to *Available.* Another hundred pounds saved there, she thought with satisfaction. What a good thing she hadn't ordered a replacement copy immediately.

Lucy smiled and piled four other books on her desk, all of which had been lost in the last year and had now turned up in the returns trolley. Unfortunately they had already been replaced, but at least they were not very expensive items and had circulated well before they had gone on AWOL, so having extra copies would do no harm.

She checked the trolley again at lunchtime as was the custom. Three more books, a couple of journals and a long lost heavy duty stapler lay helter-skelter in the cavity of the massive trolley. Evidently people didn't want to take risks with any accidentally removed library materials, not only books. The following day Lucy unearthed one library book (legitimately borrowed but slightly overdue), an old newspaper and a tattered romance with no library stamps or labels, but after that the flow stopped. Perhaps some culprits had already left the Trust and could no longer be reached by announcements placed on the intranet, or perhaps some people simply wanted to hold on to their ill-gotten gains a little longer.

Of course Infection Control was alerted – not to say alarmed – by the announcement. Their phone call was dealt with by Vlad as deputy manager in Simon's absence, but he refused to tell Lucy and Mimosa how he had managed to throw them off the scent. When Simon came back, he was pleased to see that Lucy had calmed down and apparently the precious *Principles* had been returned. He had been right, he thought; no need to make a fuss about a couple of students.

But Hector went down with measles.

TWENTY-EIGHT

THAT'S NOT A ROBIN

The plaintive tremolo of a tawny owl was heard quite distinctly by the participants of the TENNIS Cataloguing Group teleconference. Then it died away. A stunned silence followed.

"What was that?" somebody asked at last.

Mimosá hesitated, shifting uncomfortably in her chair. Should she say 'I didn't hear anything', or perhaps quite blandly 'Sounded like an owl to me'? But the meeting had only just started, so they would hear the next bird in an hour's time, and then she could hardly pretend any longer. Therefore she opted for the truth.

"It's the bird clock here at CARB," she explained as nonchalantly as she could. There was a collectively drawn breath of relief and surprise, and then laughter.

"Ah well, then we can continue with the meeting," the chairman said with an audible smile. "Your clock will come in handy if we run over time," she added.

It took Mimosa a while before she could concentrate on the meeting again. She took a sip of water and pressed her hands against her burning cheeks, then turned resolutely to the agenda. She wished the manager's office hadn't been the only place where one could attend a teleconference without disturbing (or being disturbed by) library users.

Afterwards, she recounted the incident to her colleagues. "They'll think we're all mad here," she said crossly. "Next time you win something in the staff raffle, Simon, you'd better take it home!"

"I tried," Simon reminded her, "but the family voted, and I was in the minority."

"I wonder why," Mimosa said drily.

Not everyone at the Cardigan Bay hospital was antagonistic to the library manager's bird clock. One or two library users were positively enthusiastic and wanted to know where they could buy one. Dr Achinside proudly announced a few weeks later that she had bought one and her children absolutely loved it. She only needed to mention that it would go away if they were naughty, and good behaviour was guaranteed. Simon thought a little wistfully that it didn't have that effect on his staff.

Lucy quite liked the clock, too. She secretly wished that it had been placed in their office, but it was Simon who had won it; besides, she and Mimosa received and made so many phone calls during the day that it would have been too disturbing to have them accompanied by bird sounds every hour. She tried to learn to distinguish the different birds, but Vladimir claimed it was not much use because some of them were not very life-like, for instance the nightingale.

"I've never heard a nightingale," Lucy said ruefully. "Have you?"

"Only once," Vlad said, "in Florence." He tilted his head and looked critically at the clock above Simon's desk as the next bird opened its virtual beak and sang the hour.

One day when the window in Mimosa and Lucy's office was open, they heard a cuckoo close by. "How nice," Lucy remarked, "I didn't know we had any round here." The cuckoo stopped, only to be followed by the ringing of a telephone from the trees. Both women looked perplexed, but Vlad had the answer.

"Must be a phonebill," he suggested. A more scientific explanation was provided by Simon Spindrift; he happened to be an ornithological expert besides being a Very Senior Nurse. He said a blackbird had evidently learnt to imitate not only the bird clock but also the ringtone of the telephone. Apparently this was not uncommon, though Mimosa found it hard to believe. Was there evidence of such behaviour in the literature, or was Simon Spindrift taking the mickey?

Winter time started and the clocks were duly moved back, including of course the CARB bird clock. The instructions had been lost in a fit of tidying up that had seized Simon one day, but Vlad didn't let that deter him. What was the point of having a clock if it didn't show the correct time? He took the clock down before Simon arrived, twiddled the hands for a moment and hung the clock back.

This, however, had a detrimental effect on it, as they discovered within the hour. Simon arrived together with a visitor and – like a good host – went to make a cup of tea in the staff room. Through the open door, Mimosa noticed the visitor standing and staring at the clock, which had just emitted a woodpecker's vigorous thrum.

"That's not a robin," the puzzled visitor remarked when Simon returned with the tea. He closed the door and Mimosa therefore didn't hear Simon's explanation, but she felt embarrassed on the manager's behalf. This was an important visitor, and the library should be demonstrating perfection and professionalism in every respect. She marched into Vladimir's office.

"It's your fault the clock's gone bonkers," she hissed. "You should have known better than to move the hands backwards. You should—"

"It's better this way," Vlad defended himself. "It was getting boring, at least for intelligent people like myself." He turned and picked up the phone that had conveniently started ringing, and Mimosa had to return to her desk.

Admittedly the clock had lost its novelty value and was more interesting now that they had to try and match the sound to the correct bird. They also heard calls that had previously only occurred while the library was closed. Occasionally they made a mistake of course, as that day when they closed the library an hour too early because they had heard the blue tit's call, which had previously marked five o'clock.

But Vladimir was not yet satisfied. One morning, Simon surprised him browsing an online catalogue of a company that dealt in clocks with animal sounds.

Simon opened his mouth to ask what the website could possibly have to do with the job Vlad was supposed to be doing, but the IT librarian looked up in all innocence.

"This clock will be really useful for staff management," he explained, pointing at a picture on the screen. "Look, it has a roaring lion as well as a growling tiger, both within our working hours. That way, you'll save your voice on two occasions every day. Do you think we could buy it out of the library budget?"

TWENTY-NINE

SIMON IS STRESSED

'Do you wish you had never donned the cardigan?
Do you have a vacant look about you?'

Simon Pendrive (stress on the second syllable) was sitting at his desk composing a job advertisement for the new Outreach Librarian post for Cardigan Bay Healthscare Library. He tried to think of the importance of the task, but it didn't help; so far he had only managed to write the first two sentences.

If only he didn't have such a lot to do, and if only it wasn't so noisy around him. A major refurbishment of Slouch Ward, which was located on the ground floor, had begun that morning. The first stage involved demolishing the extension that jutted out of the building just outside the library. Simon ducked instinctively when the huge bucket of an excavator swung towards him, narrowly missing the window. Why had the Powers That Be decided to refurbish the ward rather than relocate it, as they were so fond of doing? Was it because they wanted the wards on the ground floor and they had run out of suitable spaces?

He sighed, got up and went into the library office to consult a file. Lucy and Mimosa were sitting at their desks, leaning towards each other and talking in low voices. At the sight of their manager, Lucy suppressed a giggle and resumed her work. Mimosa's cheeks turned pink, and she turned away to hide it.

What was going on? Oh no, Simon thought – there is only one thing that makes women giggle and blush like that. Babies! That's the last thing a busy library manager wanted: a female colleague going on maternity leave, especially such a good worker as Lucy. Or could it be Mimosa? Or, worse still, both of them? How would Cardigan Bay Library ever survive the simultaneous absence of both Lucy and Mimosa?

Simon returned to his desk, having picked up a random file from the shelf with trembling hands. There was a bottle of water on the windowsill. He reached for it because he was thirsty, but then stopped and frowned. He never brought bottles of water into the office, so whose bottle was it? And how had it appeared there while he was out of the room for two minutes? Stepping nearer, he realised that the bottle was standing on the window ledge outside. How was that possible? Was he beginning to see things? Then the excavator swung into sight. The operator reached from the window of his cabin and neatly picked up the bottle, grinning when he noticed Simon staring at him.

A good, strong coffee would help now. Simon dropped the file on the desk and went into the staff room, where Vladimir – bless him – was making a pot. Simon sat down at the table to wait and absent-mindedly picked up an unopened packet of paper napkins. Funny, he didn't know that they had any. Hopefully Lucy hadn't bought them out of the library budget! But S-Cargo wouldn't have had them in their catalogue, he reminded himself, since they would be classified as non-essential. "Paper napkins," he read to himself, then the same in several other languages. "Serviettes.

Paperilautasliinoja." Pa—pe—ri... His head began to ache. He had a feeling there was something important he had forgotten. Somebody's birthday perhaps?

There was so much to do! If only he could put together the job advert, then Mimosa or Lucy could proofread it for him and it could be submitted; that would be one important task out of the way, and within deadline, too. Simon returned to his office and sat down at his desk again with his mug of coffee, trying to console himself with the thought that his illustrious librarian ancestors must also have been under stress and yet had survived, in even worse situations.

One word at a time, he said to himself, bringing the cursor to the desired point on the screen. One word, then another. Oh yes, he must state who the new person would report to.

A pneumatic drill sprang into action seconds before the phone rang. Simon picked up the receiver, but couldn't hear a word. He roared, "Library," down the line and thought he could distinguish "What did you say?" coming from the other end. He slammed the phone down and took a sip out of his mug. His teeth rattled against it as the drilling went on. Then he turned resolutely to his computer again, wondering if the keys might be shaken out at this rate.

'We're a small but vibrant library service.' That was good; that would attract the right kind of applicants. But why hadn't the builders warned them how noisy the work would be? It was outrageous. Yes, that was the word: outrageous!

***

An hour later, Simon Pendrive (stress in every corner of his brain) finally printed out a draft version of the job advertisement and took it to Lucy as the most conscientious member of his team.

"Lucy," he roared, trying to make himself heard as the wall of the extension began to tumble. A cloud of dust obscured the daylight. "Here's a draft version of the advert for the Outreach Librarian's post. Can you proofread it for me, please? Now?"

Lucy nodded in agreement, coughing because some of the dust had managed to get inside, and took the paper. Simon was sure that she was looking guilty. What on earth was going on here? He went back into his office and buried his aching head in his hands, nearly dipping his nose in the coffee mug.

When Lucy looked in after a few minutes, the noise had stopped because the workmen had taken a break, but Simon still sat slumped at his desk. Lucy felt sorry for him. There was so much to do and not enough staff to do it. Hopefully the situation would improve once they had the Outreach Librarian in place. She had to tap Simon on the shoulder to draw his attention to the paper she was offering him.

"It's a really good job advert, Simon," Lucy said encouragingly. "A few minor corrections, though." Simon groaned and snatched the paper from Lucy's hand. What was this? Had he really said they were *a small, vibrant building site library?*

"You've written *reports to the library serviettes manager,*" she said. "You must have meant..." Simon groaned again and opened the file on his computer to make the corrections.

"Then you keep referring to the *outrage librarian,*" Lucy went on. "I'm sure you meant—"

Simon began to gnash his teeth and bang his fist on the desk. He wanted to pound those words out of the sheet of paper. He aimed carefully at the lines that said *Libraries are no longer needed – you can find it all on Google. Ideally, candidates should have no previous experience of working in a library.*

He didn't get as far as the words *Interviews will be held wherever the library happens to be located at the time,* because the banging had alerted Mimosa, who now appeared at the door. Simon turned round to face her. There it was again, that look of complicity! Which of them was it? When would she start her maternity leave? How was the library going to cope? And incidentally, who on earth was Mimosa's partner?

Mimosa spoke calmly and with determination. "Come, Simon, there is something in the staff room we must show you."

"Not now," Simon wailed. "There's so much to do!"

"That's right," Lucy chimed in. "That's why you've got to come *now*, it's something you must prioritise."

Together they led the moaning manager into the staff room, where Vlad was ready with more coffee and a large cream cake. Cups and plates and paper napkins were arranged on the table, and the usual clutter of library journals had been tidied away.

"Happy birthday, Simon!" he said, handing Simon a card which bore their good wishes. "We thought you might forget it was your birthday as you're so busy, so we decided to surprise you. I was worried Lucy and Mimosa would give the game away though, they've been whispering together all morning. Come and cut the cake now!"

And so he did, while his colleagues burst into a vigorous but slightly unmusical rendering of *Happy Birthday to You.*

THIRTY

ENTER CRISPIN

The selection process for the new outreach librarian was at last completed. They had had fewer applications than Simon had hoped for, at least from people who fulfilled the requirements for the post. The job advertisement had clearly stated that an experienced, qualified librarian was wanted; after his ghastly experience of trying to put together the advert when stressed, Simon had asked both Vladimir and Mimosa to proofread the new version for him, so he knew this requirement had been made explicit. Nevertheless, one applicant stated she had qualified and worked as a neuropsychiatrist in her country of origin, another one had trained as a hairdresser, and a third one had experience in grooming horses. None of these three had any library qualifications or experience of working in a library. A couple of applicants who had worked as Saturday volunteers doing shelving in their local libraries were at least on the right track, more so than the applicant who had shelving experience in a supermarket only.

Vladimir had been away when the interviews took place and had therefore not met any of the candidates. Thus when Crispin Curlewe entered the Healthscare Library on the first morning after his appointment, the IT librarian realised he wasn't ready to meet this cheerful and pleasant looking young man so suddenly. Crispin was not very tall, his hair was sand coloured and curly, and he had slightly round features and a ready but relaxed smile.

They all gathered round a pot of coffee in the staff room for a start. "I remember you," Crispin said, turning to Lucy. "You showed me round after the interview."

Vlad glowered. Why should the intruder – sorry, the newcomer – remember Lucy in particular? Why not Mimosa? And why did Lucy smile so sweetly in response? Vlad was still suspicious of people who smiled responsively as he hadn't reached that stage in his new skill yet. Damn it, he thought, I'll have to practise if I'm to keep up. But it was absurd to bare one's teeth whenever one wanted to indicate one's friendliness. Dogs didn't do it, so why should people?

It had been agreed beforehand that after Simon had dealt with the manager's part of the induction and the paperwork, each team member would be involved in showing Crispin the ropes. This would ensure that he would settle in more quickly and that the whole team would share the responsibility. So, halfway through the morning and the second pot of coffee, Crispin knocked on Vlad's open door and stepped in.

"Simon says you and I will share this office," Crispin announced, looking around. "I know," Vlad answered curtly. This of course was the ultimate annoyance. Why should *he* share his office and not Simon? Vlad made a mental note to get a few drawing pins from the stationery cupboard. Just a couple would do; they could be dropped on Crispin's chair in a way that looked accidental. Then he turned back to his work while the outreach librarian began to sort out the things he wanted on his desk; a computer had already been delivered the day before.

"I like your fiancée," Crispin continued. "I'm sure she would get on with my girlfriend."

Vladimir's shoulders relaxed a little at the word 'girlfriend', but he didn't say anything. Let the other man chatter away – he, Vlad, had work to do. Crispin would find out soon enough that everyone had plenty to do in this establishment, with little time to spare for pleasantries. Being a librarian wasn't just a nice little job like some people seemed to think.

Crispin reached under the desk, where he had noticed a small, pastel coloured object. "What's this, Vladimir?" he asked, holding a dainty three-dimensional paper star in his hand. Vlad was forced to turn round (only by a few carefully judged degrees of course) in order to see what the other man was talking about. It was one of his 3D paper stars, their Christmas decorations, which had fallen under the desk and had escaped the cleaner. Vlad muttered an explanation and turned back to his computer again.

Crispin held the star very carefully in his fingers and examined it. "It's fantastic. Who made it? Or do you all know how to make them? Is it part of the requirements for working here?" He laughed a little.

Vlad's shoulders relaxed slightly more this time. He turned round again in his chair to face Crispin. "It must be one of mine," he said. "I've tried to show the others how to make them, but Mimosa is no good at all and Simon won't even try. Lucy is the only one who could produce a decent star, but she needs to practise."

"I'm sure the instructions are on the web," Crispin said enthusiastically, switching his PC on. Vlad's shoulders stiffened immediately, and he bent over his computer almost protectively. "It's not as easy as you think," he grunted.

"Of course it would be better if you showed me how," Crispin said. "I'm sure I could learn it, I'm quite good at knitting complicated patterns."

Vlad sat up instantly and stared at his new colleague. It was only now that he noticed the sweater the other man was wearing. It had a complicated but pleasantly artistic pattern – kind of folksy – so was it possible that this guy knitted his own sweaters? Wait till Mimosa hears this, Vlad thought with some malice. She would be impressed, but would of course pretend that knitting was the most natural thing in the world for a man to do, as much as for a woman, except that she probably couldn't knit to save her life. Vlad had tried a few times and had got as far as ribbing, but that wasn't enough if one wanted to knit a pair of socks. And a pair of socks was what he really wanted, because walking socks were expensive and in any case bought socks were unsatisfactory compared with hand knitted woollen ones. What if...

Half an hour later, the library manager passed Vlad and Crispin's office. He stopped and listened at the open door for a moment, pretending to be studying a poster that Lucy had put up. Those two seemed to be getting on with each other. What a relief; he had been worried about Vlad's reaction. But Simon realised now how out of touch he was with current trends. He had never known that an outreach service or any IT related issue would involve something called ribbing. He would really have to catch up with all this modern terminology one of these days.

THIRTY-ONE

A MUG'S GAME

Crispin was sitting in Simon's office. He had the unpleasant task of reporting to his manager that he hadn't been able to get to the library promotion at Knowl Edge on time, and so the local team had had to call the whole thing off after waiting for him in vain for an hour.

"I couldn't find the place, and by the time I'd finally got there—"

"What do you mean, couldn't find the place? Haven't you got satnav in your car?" Simon wanted to know.

"No, only a map," Crispin said ruefully. "Do you think the library could pay for a satnav if I had it installed?"

"Certainly not," Simon said indignantly. "How come you couldn't read the map if you had one? All you have to do is to get yourself to where the Straits of Dire come into view, then turn right, and there you are. And why did it take you so long to get back here?" Expression 3B was developing on the library manager's features.

"Well, I thought I might as well drop in at the Crown and Bridge for an early lunch. Vlad says the food is much better than in the staff canteen here and the dentists all go there, so..."

"That's enough!" Simon interrupted. "Now you must plan your promo schedule again and fit in Knowl Edge somehow. I want to see the updated plan first thing tomorrow." With that, he turned and stomped out of the room - quite forgetting that he had always thought stomping was beneath him - and went in search of his favourite coffee receptacle and, of course, something to fill it with. But the mug wasn't in the staff room. He returned to his office, but it wasn't on the desk or on the windowsill. He spent a good ten minutes going through every possible hiding place there. Then he checked the kitchenette next to the library where they always did their washing up, spending another ten minutes opening and shutting cupboards (each one twice, just in case), each time with a slightly louder bang.

Hopeless. The mug was nowhere to be seen. Mimosa came in to fill the kettle and heard the sad news. She sympathised; she knew that Simon was very fond of his mug. It was green and white and had a picture of a tennis racket on it, with the acronym TENNIS and the URL of the regional libraries' website. Somebody must have fancied it and taken it when it was accidentally left behind in the kitchenette. They wouldn't have known that TENNIS stood for The Electronic Nearly National Information System and had nothing whatsoever to do with the sport.

"Never mind," Simon said bravely but sadly, "I'll have my coffee out of whatever cup is available, then."

Crispin heard the story and decided it was time to make amends, having failed his first promo trip so dismally. He therefore abandoned the update to his promotional schedule that he was supposed to be doing and started an internet search instead.

Mimosa also decided to take action. She had an old TENNIS coaster in her desk drawer, and she took a colour photocopy of it. She wrote a message under the picture in large letters and stuck the paper on one of the cupboard doors in the kitchenette. Then she returned to her office and started waiting for results. There was a long list of book suggestions from Dr Terremoto to assess for purchase; just the thing to tackle on a day like this.

Before Simon had finished his first coffee from an anonymous but capacious cup, Jill the medical secretary walked into the library office with the beloved green and white mug.

"I don't know whose this is," she said to Mimosa, proffering the mug. "But I was in the kitchenette checking the milk situation and saw a notice that a mug with this picture had gone missing, and I knew that one of the junior doctors had it in his office. I know, because I was there this morning. So I went in and told him that it wasn't his to take away. Look, I've even washed it. And I've taken down your notice since it's no longer needed."

Mimosa got up and took the mug. "Thanks, Jill," she said with more warmth than she usually displayed when talking to Jill. "It's Simon's favourite, and he was really upset when it went missing. I'll tell him it was you who found it."

She filled the mug and brought it to Simon together with the story. The things we do here in this place, she said to herself – but looking for a lost mug was a change from looking for lost books. It was good to see Simon's eyes light up when he saw his treasure.

A few days later, the post brought a shapeless parcel marked for the attention of Simon Pendrive, Library Services

Manager. The sender's label was almost illegible, and Lucy was worried there might be a bomb or some noxious material in the parcel, but Mimosa pointed out that no one was likely to want to harm Simon. It was probably some online catalogue company whose labels were printed cheaply and didn't last the journey. Lucy therefore took the parcel in to Simon, who opened it with some difficulty as there were multiple layers of bubble wrap. He handed those to Lucy to be kept for covering cracks in the windows in winter (the Great Refurb hadn't included new window frames) and peeled off the tissue paper that covered the object. It was a large white mug that said THE MANAGER IS ALWAYS RIGHT in bright red capital letters. Inside the mug there was a folded delivery note which bore the message, 'Message to recipient: Hope you'll enjoy your coffee again. Crispin.'

Of course Simon had to parade his new mug and drink a celebratory coffee out of it to show how much he appreciated it. He felt he had been too harsh to Crispin about his miscarried promo trip; after all, the man didn't know the area and it was his first outreach trip. He would simply have to prepare his next trip properly.

"So, that's what you did all Friday afternoon!" Vladimir exclaimed. "I was wondering what you were doing, looking at all those gift websites." He grinned at Crispin, who turned pink and cast a sideways glance at Simon. But Simon pretended he hadn't heard Vlad's indiscreet comment. He had two mugs now, an old one and a new one. He looked from one to the other. One mug was half full, one was half empty. Life was in balance.

THIRTY-TWO

ON THE CARPET

Adonis shut the door of the reading room behind him, nearly trapping the flex of the vacuum cleaner. He went to find the library manager, pulling the vac behind him like a child's toy.

"I'm tired of your customers who bring in messy food," he announced, standing at the door of Simon's office. It sounded like a declaration of war. "Too many crumbs on the carpet. Too many fingerprints on the computers. Too much sticky Coke on the table. It must stop!"

Simon explained patiently that they had already tried polite notices and posters as well as pointing out to offending users that they weren't allowed to bring food or drink into the reading room, but Adonis snorted and turned to go out. He got tangled in the vacuum cleaner flex, but Simon pretended to be busy and didn't get up to help; he thought Adonis looked ready to bite even a helping hand.

The matter of food and drink was of course a perennial problem, and one which was frequently and thoroughly aired on the medical librarians' email discussion list. Simon was usually very philosophical and tried to prove that it was a question of choice: they had to choose which more important, having happy users and a bit of mess, or having unhappy users – or worse still, no users – and a clean library.

True, some kinds of behaviour were definitely problematic, such as knocking over a coffee cup while sitting at a keyboard. This had happened to a reader recently, and the unfortunate girl had admitted that her mother had recently had a similar accident at home. No lessons learnt there...

But there was so much to do in the Healthscare Library – even now that they had another member in the team – that there really wasn't much time to think about customers' feeding problems. Right now, Simon was busy trying to find out why there was a persistent rumour going round that the library would be relocated into the space currently occupied by the Trust switchboard. In any case Adonis seemed to be the one who suffered most from the food and drink situation since he was the one who had to deal with the mess, and he was going on leave for a fortnight.

The absence of Adonis, however, didn't simply create a breathing space. In fact it almost literally deprived the library of it, because the temporary cleaner sprayed all the surfaces lavishly with furniture polish, something that they had had to ask Adonis not to do because a few sensitive readers had complained. But they didn't want to scare the temp away completely in case the next one did something even worse. The very first one hadn't emptied the bin in the staff room or vacuum cleaned in there. When the smell began to spread along the corridor and it was reported to Facilities as a possible gas leak, Simon finally asked the cleaner why she hadn't dealt with the staff room. The answer was simple: she hadn't dared enter because it said LIBRARY STAFF ONLY on the door.

"Crisps are also food," Mimosa remarked acidly to a reader who had spent the best part of an hour crunching away at the contents of a giant bag of salt and vinegar crisps while writing a report at a computer in the reading room. The reader looked up in surprise, brushed the crumbs from the workstation onto the floor and wiped his greasy fingers in his sweater. Mimosa pointedly asked him to move away from the workstation so that the cleaner could tidy it up. The reader collected his papers and looked with interest at the sticker that was now revealed. It bore the message: "No food or drink at this workstation." "I didn't see that sticker," he explained to Mimosa. "It was under my papers."

The dutiful temp came in, pulled up the vacuum cleaner, sucked away the remaining crumbs and a couple of loose keys from the keyboard, and squirted window cleaning fluid on the computer screen. Mimosa snatched the bottle from his hand.

"But you told me not to use furniture polish," the offended cleaner reminded her. In the meantime the reader had abandoned all hope of finishing his report and went instead to complain to the library manager that he hadn't been allowed to work in peace.

Seething with impotent rage, Mimosa returned to her office and recounted to Lucy the latest in the food and drink saga. Lucy felt guilty because she had been eating and drinking at her workstation. Perhaps it set a bad example to their customers? Crispin, who happened to be in the office, pointed out that since they weren't allowed more than one coffee break, they had to refresh themselves at their desks. "We're tied to our desks, you know," he said, twirling the end of Lucy's scarf as if to tie her to her desk with it.

Crispin repeated the phrase to Vladimir, whose eyes flashed with that "I-have-an-idea" kind of flash that Simon had come to dread. But Simon, like Adonis, had gone on a fortnight's annual leave and thus wasn't there to witness his deputy's brainwave.

For the next hour or so, Crispin and Vladimir were closeted in their office. Then they emerged and triumphantly dragged the noticeboard stand to the reading room entrance and pinned a large notice on it.

"This should do it," Vlad announced. "We'll see if it doesn't bring the blighters to heel."

The message read in large red letters: NIL BY MOUTH.

It seemed that Vlad had overestimated the power that their notice would have on their disobedient customers. The first day was a success, but then a few readers began to sneak their coffee cups and sandwiches in again, and after the weekend the waste bin was overflowing with the remains of several snacks and lunches. Then Dr Achinside saw the notice, turned on her heels and walked out. The men were pleased with her reaction, but Lucy thought there was something ominous about the way the doctor had frowned.

"Status quo ante," Crispin sighed. "We'll have to think again."

"I have already done so," Vlad grinned. "You look after the shop, ladies, Cris and I have something important to do." And they shut their office door behind them before Mimosa had time to protest.

***

Simon had a quick look at his work emails the evening before his return from holiday. A manager could never leave his emails for too long, he said to himself with a delightfully self-important feeling that was tinged with regret. His illustrious librarian ancestors could have had no idea what life was like when one was constantly bombarded with messages that had to be responded to at short notice. Then Simon bit his lip. What had his staff been up to? There was a stiff message from Dr Achinside and another one from Simon Spindrift, which also amounted to a complaint... and what was this email from a medical student? He complained because all he had done was to order a pizza to be delivered to the library – he was preparing for an exam, he didn't have time to eat out – but one of the librarians (the tall one) had intercepted and confiscated it.

***

Simon got off his trusty old bicycle the following morning and approached his library with a sense of gloom. Why did he have to go on leave? He had to guard the place constantly. He could not be expected to conform to the norms that ordinary employees had to conform to, and he would have to discuss the matter with his line manager – and with his wife, of course. She would understand.

He opened the door of the Healthscare Library, and the noticeboard stand greeted him in the lobby with a poster that stated:

LIBRARY RULES

No food or drink is allowed anywhere in the library. Alternatively, only nice food and drink is allowed in the library, because:

Any food or drink brought into the library must be shared with library staff

Any food or drink brought into the library and not willingly shared will be confiscated by library staff

NB1 Crisps are also food

NB2 It is forbidden to use your sandwich as a bookmark

NB3 These rules do not apply to library staff since they are tied to their desks

To illustrate the last point, there was a photo of Crispin tied not only to his desk but also his chair.

Adonis returned from his holiday the same day. Unlike Simon, he was happy: there were no more crumbs on the carpet in the reading room. But two members of library staff were on the carpet in the library manager's office.

THIRTY-THREE

TRUST ME, I'M A LIBRARIAN

Vladimir was sitting in the hospital café one day, idly flicking through the pages of a newspaper. At a nearby table two nurses were comparing experiences of some new software the Trust had recently adopted for patient records, and the IT librarian's interest was naturally aroused.

"It took me ages this morning to enter Mr—I mean, a certain new patient's details because he wouldn't disclose whether he had a pet or not," one nurse complained. "Then I had to ask him what type of house he had, but nothing would fit the alternatives."

"Tell me about it," the other one sighed. "Maisonette, chalet, apartment, mobile home, you name it – it's all American, that's the problem. As for pets, I don't understand the point of recording them if you've only come to hospital for a knee operation. I mean, it makes sense if you're suffering from allergies, but how can your pet affect your knee problems? And if somebody says they've got a towzy tyke, how on earth do I know whether to tick the box for Furred or Smooth?"

"Well, housing might be relevant to the patient's knee op, but what about that patient who had a problem with her denture? She had to disclose that she lived in a stately home but they only used the west wing because of the damp, so the nurse didn't know what to do and selected Vulnerably housed," the first nurse said. "I heard it from my friend Sally, so it must be true," she added when her colleague looked incredulous.

A man in overalls, who was sitting at the next table, now leaned over to join the conversation.

"Never mind your patients, I'm an electrician, and I was asked whether I was single, married or divorced when I went to deal with a faulty light switch in the Physio department. Couldn't fill in the form otherwise, they said. I said what form, I have a ticket from the Estates, but they wouldn't hear any of it."

Vlad felt a twinge of envy. The sparkie was very handsome, so perhaps the Physio receptionist had used the opportunity to find out whether he was available or not.

"I know, that's where I work. I think they've mixed the software up somehow and got the wrong version for the wrong department," the first nurse said with a knowledgeable air.

Vlad threw the newspaper on the table and jumped up so that the nurses turned round, startled. The café was nearly empty, and it suddenly crossed their minds that they might have been talking too freely and been overheard. Oh dear... why had that tall man jumped up like that? Had they said something untoward? But they hadn't mentioned any patient names or any other confidential information, and neither had the electrician.

The IT librarian returned to the library with glowing eyes. He would solve these problems by adapting the software to British circumstances as well as correcting any compatibility problems, and that would save the Trust no end of money because it would save so much staff time. It would impress Simon, and Lucy of course. It could always be made evidence based by keeping a record of... His thoughts ran ahead, so that he bumped into Mimosa when he swung the door of the library open. Ah, but he would have to be cunning, otherwise Simon might say no. Simon had an unpleasant habit of saying no to many of his suggestions.

Vlad suddenly turned his inward gaze out and noticed Mimosa, whose elbow he had bashed with the door handle. He muttered an apology, brushed past her and walked briskly into the manager's office.

"Simon, I need to visit one of the wards urgently where they've implemented the new patient record software," he started. "I – I've been asked, I mean I'd like to, erm, watch them use it, but I'm not sure they'll let me do it without your permission as it will dis—display patient data." His words ran out fast. It was like that time when, as a young boy, he had run down a steep hill and his feet had started running faster and faster until he lost his balance.

"And why would you need to see this new software so urgently?" the library manager asked drily. This didn't bode well; Vlad was up to no good. Simon tilted his head slightly and looked at Vlad over his glasses, a gesture which he had adopted recently and with which he was very satisfied.

"Um, I want to ad—I mean, imp—" Vlad's heart sank. He couldn't tell an outright lie. Damn it, he hadn't thought about his strategy sufficiently. He should have taken more time before asking for permission; now he had only succeeded in making Simon suspicious.

Mimosa, who had followed Vlad, had an answer. "He wants to mess around with their software, that's what it is," she declared crossly, rubbing her elbow as a reminder, although it had almost stopped hurting. Simon laughed at what he took to be a joke. "Haven't you got enough to do with your FROSTBITE project? There's software enough and to share before it's all up and running."

"Oh, I've given up on FROSTBITE," Vladimir said airily. "Lucy can get on with her interlibrary loans without it. And so can the rest of the world, I don't think it's a viable proposition after all. I want to have a look at that new—"

Simon realised this wasn't a joke. Goodness, it could have serious consequences if Vlad really managed to gain access to one of the wards and started playing around with their software! It *would* have serious consequences. He might accidentally (or worse still, on purpose) alter or lose patient data – and viewing it was bad enough anyway. Anything could happen. Simon gathered his brows and put on his most convincing Expression 3B.

"You will *not* do it, Vladimir. I will not give you my permission, and you will not try to gain access by any other means," he said sternly.

"But those poor nurses are in distress! Other people are having problems, too! I heard them talking about it in the café," Vlad protested.

Mimosa stepped out from behind him. "There! I knew you were planning something stupid! I guessed right!" she shouted triumphantly.

"And who asked you to interfere?" Vlad snapped back. Really, the woman was intolerable. Why didn't Simon keep her in order? Then Lucy emerged from her office, looking anxiously at her colleagues' faces. What was going on? It sounded worse than usual. But she would defend Vlad, whatever had happened or was about to happen.

A fresh breeze of discord was blowing through the Healthscare Library.

The following day, Vlad mentioned he would go downstairs for his lunch. The others didn't take much notice since there was nothing unusual about that – a routine announcement, that was all. On the way down he met Crispin, who asked to borrow Vlad's access badge because he had forgotten his own.

"Please, Vlad! I know we're not supposed to do it, but Mimosa was so cross with me this morning when she had to let me in," Crispin pleaded. "I'll bring it back straight away, I promise."

Vladimir extracted his staff badge from his pocket and shoved it in the other man's hand. Cris was a good guy, but sometimes apt to be forgetful, he thought as he walked on towards – no, not the café where lunch was waiting, but the Physiotherapy department. There he had a bit of luck because he met a consultant who knew him and who was just coming out, so he was able to slip in without attracting attention.

But Vlad's joy was short lived. He had barely managed to sneak behind the receptionist's counter when he recognised one of the nurses who had complained about the software the day before.

"Hello," the IT librarian said as cheerfully as he knew how. This is where a smile would have come in handy, he thought, regretting that he had neglected his exercises. "I've come to have a look at your new software. I hear you've been having problems with it." He slid towards the PC, which was standing on the desk – unlocked, inviting.

The nurse eyed him suspiciously. Wasn't that the man who had behaved so strangely in the café yesterday? He wore no staff badge, so he was probably a patient or a visitor. Or a thief! There had been warnings issued lately on the Trust intranet about thieves. She challenged Vlad to show his badge, standing between him and the way out.

"I haven't got my badge, I lent it to a friend," he said a little feebly.

"Oh yes, and haven't you read the message from the security officer about lending your badge to others?" The nurse's voice was a shade firmer now.

"I know, but... I'm the IT librarian, I only want to—" Vlad tried, tapping at the keyboard to keep it from locking. The nurse's brows formed a dark V shape.

"Never heard of an IT librarian. It's up to the IT department to look at computers, not the library. What's your name?"

"Logoff," Vlad said, swallowing hard. What would the nurse do now? Call Security? But he only needed to phone the library, they would vouch for him. Or... what if Simon answered and heard that he, Vlad, was at the Physio department? He would guess immediately the reason for the visit. Poor Vlad imagined himself in his line manager's office, and beads of perspiration began to run down his forehead.

"No, I won't log off," the nurse said rather crossly. "I'll call Security now since you can't account for yourself." She reached over the counter and picked up the receiver. Vlad pushed aside the chair he had instinctively placed between himself and the nurse, and ran.

It was only in the corridor that he remembered that there were no security men on site any longer. He drew a deep breath to steady himself and walked into the café with a deliberately casual step. It would take some time before a security man arrived from Backwater, and by that time he would have returned to the library and got his staff badge back from Crispin. He picked up a sandwich, paid for it, and hoped that the colleague answering the doorbell wouldn't be Mimosa. This would be the last time he let Crispin borrow his badge, he promised himself as he pressed the intercom button at the bottom of the stairs.

"Hi, it's Vlad," he said. He had to repeat it because the intercom crackled just at that moment. "Librarian," he added.

"Oh yes, that's what they all say," came Mimosa's reply coldly. Then there was a click, and the phone went quiet.

"Ring Security, somebody," Mimosa called out to her colleagues. "The man who tried to gain access to the Physio department is trying to come up to the library now. Says he's a librarian. I hope Vlad doesn't let him in by accident when he comes back from lunch. I wonder where he is, incidentally? He should have been back by now."

THIRTY-FOUR

JACK THE READER STRIKES AGAIN

Things were always a little fraught when one of the CARB team was about to go on leave. There were last minute jobs to be completed, instructions to be given to colleagues and the out-of-office message to be set on emails. On the following day the rest of the team would at first feel as if their hair had been cut shorter than usual or a tooth had been removed, leaving a gap. At the same time they would feel relieved because the distraught staff member was now on holiday and the rest of them could carry on without being constantly interrupted with urgent queries and advice.

This was exactly how things were after Simon had finally departed for the library conference. For about a fortnight there had been talk only of the conference, and of the paper Simon would read there. Of course, he had had to make sure that the Healthscare Library was prepared for his absence for a whole week, all the more so since Crispin was away as well so they would be short staffed by two members. But the library manager seemed to have forgotten that the team was deprived of his lead every time he went on holiday, and so they knew pretty well by now what to expect and what their tasks were in this situation.

The two ladies breathed a sigh of relief on the first day of Simon's absence, but Vlad rubbed his hands together with delight. Once again, he had a chance of being in charge. This time he would really make sure some changes took place – and for the better.

He stepped into the library office, ready to announce his plan of improvements. To his dismay, he found his fiancée sobbing her heart out and Mimosa trying in vain to comfort her.

"I know they're only books," Lucy wailed. "But I can't bear it."

"They're not 'only' books, Lucy," Mimosa said with warmth. "I get upset, too, when they disappear. They represent a lot of hard work on our part. They've cost the library a lot because of our input, not only because of the money that was paid for them. And of course our users want the books, so every time somebody asks for a book that's walked, we have to decide what to do. So it's not surprising you're upset, though I wish you'd be a bit more professional about it."

She drew breath and turned to Vladimir, who had stopped at the door.

"Mr Cutter was here asking for three books, but they've all disappeared, every one of them. This is in addition to two books going AWOL from the new titles display only a few days ago. We're at our wits' end what to do – it's going to cost a lot to replace all five books, and the three that Mr Cutter needs urgently must still be requested on interlibrary loan in the interim," she reported. "You're the deputy manager, you should do something," she added crossly.

Lucy burst into tears again and was gently ushered into the staff room by Vlad.

"It seems it wasn't enough when Lucy alerted people that a contaminated book had been stolen," he said on his return to the office. "Or else these are new users who have never heard the story. I agree we've got to take action. You put the coffee on and I'll think of something."

For once, Mimosa didn't protest when Vlad gave her orders. She went into the staff room, switched the kettle on so that Lucy could have a calming cup of camomile tea, and started to make a pot of coffee for herself and Vlad. If a user had turned up with a missing book just then, Mimosa would have taken action which she would have had to regret afterwards. It was a miracle she didn't break the coffee pot with her aggressive handling. As to the amount of coffee she measured into the filter, it would have been enough to poison anyone.

"It's Jack the Reader again," she muttered as she switched the machine on and went to the reading room to check for the third time that the books Mr Cutter wanted hadn't somehow miraculously crept back into the section on surgery.

Jack the Reader was the imaginary character they had accidentally invented one day. Vladimir had taken a call from somebody who was asking for a book by Jack de Reader – or so Vlad claimed when he had to ask Mimosa for help because he had never heard of such an author. He wasn't sure if it was 'de' or 'the' Reader because of the caller's accent, but he wasn't at all cheered by Mimosa's explanation that they must have meant Jacques Derrida, the philosopher, whose name admittedly was usually pronounced with the stress on the last syllable.

"Derry-dah," Mimosa demonstrated.

"Derry-down-dilly," Vlad retorted and returned to his office, where the caller was still waiting at the other end of the line.

"You could have said thank you," Mimosa shouted after him, but he either didn't hear or didn't want to. But from that day, Jack the Reader was the one they all blamed when something went wrong inexplicably.

The day they discovered the loss of three books on surgery, they agreed ruefully that it must have been Jack the Reader's doing. This didn't console them much though. Two pots of coffee were consumed before any of them felt better, and that was just between Mimosa and Vladimir since Lucy only drank camomile tea.

"Chained libraries, that's the answer," Vlad said suddenly. "Your turn to make the next pot, Samosa."

Mimosa gritted her teeth and decided for once not to retaliate; they had enough trouble being short staffed and having to conjure up books to replace the missing ones. She therefore picked up the coffee pot obediently. Lucy didn't know what chained libraries were, so Vlad explained to her how in the distant past, books in monastic libraries had been chained to shelves so that they could not be removed. Satisfied with this, Lucy continued to source Mr Cutter's books from other libraries, and Vladimir shut himself in his office. He only reappeared briefly to ask Mimosa how many running metres of books they had, then how many volumes they had, then how many of them were worth more than £10 (most of them were, of course) and finally to ask Lucy to lend him a copy of the NHS Cargo catalogue. The ladies looked at each other every time, more and more mystified.

At the end of the day they had the answer to their unspoken question. Vlad had ordered enough chain (with small links, plus the necessary screws and bolts) to fasten all of the books worth more than £10 to the shelves.

"And who's going to do the fixing?" Mimosa asked. "Al Monte?"

"Of course, it's the Estates' job to set things up. Either Al or one of his colleagues if he's on leave. It counts as a New Work, but I can sign for that, don't you worry," Vlad reassured Mimosa, having guessed her next question.

Lucy was surprised to hear that Vlad had found a suitable product in S-Cargo's catalogue, but actually why not? The Estates had to do all kinds of jobs that might require chains of various lengths and thicknesses, and they would have to order everything from S-Cargo like anybody else. The pigeon chains that had been fixed on the windows must have been supplied by S-Cargo, not by a local ironmonger (had one still existed).

They were all busy for the next two days. Mimosa rewrote the loans policy to accommodate the fact that books could no longer be taken out of the library; Vlad worded a message to that effect to be emailed to all their customers; Lucy designed several large posters to be displayed in the library to explain the new policy and to apologise for any inconvenience caused while the installation work was ongoing.

On the third morning, a large cardboard box addressed to the library was standing in a corner of the Reception area when Lucy came in. It must be the chains, Lucy thought as the receptionist handed her the post, and a little shiver of excitement ran along her spine. What would the library look like once the work was completed? How long would it take? She hurried upstairs, and as soon as Vlad appeared, she asked him to collect the parcel as she didn't think she could move it herself.

Vlad came back quickly, carrying the parcel, but he didn't look as happy as the others had expected. He threw the box down on the floor of the lobby, and they all gathered around it.

"It's too light," he announced sombrely. "Something must be wrong. It's that S-Cargo again."

Mimosa gave the box a cautious push and was surprised that it moved quite easily. Vlad tore it open so violently that Lucy was worried he might cut himself, but she didn't dare say a word while he was in that mood. There was a lot of packing material as usual, but in the end it was all removed (and scattered all over the floor). What was left was several hundred packs of strips for making paper chains, gummed, in assorted colours.

Vlad straightened himself and looked at the two women without saying anything for a while. The phone rang in the office, but no one moved. Then at last he said: "It's their mistake. I'll give them a ring and a piece of my mind. I bet they'll say it can't be returned, or something equally stupid."

"I'll make some coffee," Mimosa said and disappeared into the staff room.

Through the half open door of Vlad's office, Lucy could distinguish a torrent of swear words in several languages, the like of which had never been heard in the Healthscare Library. She was full of admiration but also a little scared: what if S-Cargo complained to Simon about Vlad's swearing?

"Just as I thought," he said bitterly, having slammed the phone down and emerged from his office. "They said paper chains were cheaper than metal ones and they always have to source the cheapest product. We can't return them." He gave the box a good kick, then started to jump on the packing materials until they'd all been flattened.

"Hey, wait a minute, Vlad!" Mimosa protested as she came out of the staff room. "Why didn't you leave any for us? We want to let off steam, too!" At that moment, the entrance door opened and Victor A. Moose entered, so they all had to calm down and pick up the wreckage. It wouldn't do to let Claire Twinsett's PA see the library in a mess. Lucy dragged the box into their office, wondering how they could dispose of paper chain materials amounting to hundreds of metres. It was too much for the library, and in any case they had plenty of paper chains left from that Christmas decoration competition that they had won.

But Vlad hadn't given up. He retired once more into his office with a mug of coffee. On his return, he looked determined but almost pleased. "I'll drive down to Knowl Edge," he said briefly, scooping up the now somewhat battered cardboard box in his arms.

"Whatever for?" Mimosa wondered.

"Children's Services," was the reply. The two ladies smiled with delight and set to work, Mimosa to return the loans policy to its original wording and Lucy to delete the poster documents she had created. They would find a way of beating Jack the Reader some other way. For the moment, they were pleased to see the last of those paper chain packages and didn't want to hear about them ever again.

THIRTY-FIVE

GAMES PEOPLE PLAY

Heathrow Airport. Simon Pendrive proceeds through the green lane at Arrivals and towards the area where passengers are being met. As he emerges into the lounge, crowds of people behind the cordon crane their necks eagerly. A Salvation Army band sitting on the left is playing for all they're worth in honour of the occasion.

Simon's throat is momentarily constricted with emotion. Never before has he been greeted with marching music and by excited crowds. How did they know to expect his arrival from the library conference? The news of his successful paper must have reached the media and made an impression, even though Simon himself has not heard anything about it on the news nor seen any headlines.

He adjusts the coat which is hanging over his arm, and tries to look modest and natural as he walks past the crowds. It's difficult when you're not used to it. He has performed in public many times, but only as a member of a choir and never on his own, not even as a soloist. This is a moment that not even the most renowned of his librarian ancestors can possibly have experienced.

Then Simon is brought down to earth again – no pun intended, even though his plane has landed. He notices there are men and women here and there wearing identical pink T-shirts, and he remembers what day it is: the day before the start of the London Olympic Games. He sighs and is glad that he hasn't waved or nodded to any of the onlookers, but he does nod encouragingly to a group of fellow passengers who judging by their outfits are part of some foreign athletic team. Then he threads his way out of the arrivals area and into the Central Bus Station.

***

Back in the library the following day, Simon found his team busy. Mainly they were busy sulking, but this couldn't have been called a team effort since they all had their various reasons and were practising in different locations albeit simultaneously. Lucy was sulking because Vladimir hadn't bought her five rings in spite of her suggestion that it would have been appropriate in honour of the Olympics. Mimosa was sulking because she had no one who would have bought her even one ring. Vlad was sulking because he couldn't watch the Games but had to plan his library training programme for the autumn. Last but not least, Crispin was sulking because he had returned from his holidays just at the beginning of the Games and thus couldn't watch them but had to plan his outreach programme.

Eventually, Vlad and Crispin discovered that their sulk had the same origin, and from there it was only a short step to taking action.

About mid-morning, a new notice appeared on the shared electronic team calendar. Vladimir and Crispin were both booked on to a teleconference with one of the groups in the

TENNIS libraries' network, and the session was to begin immediately. Mimosa was annoyed because such a sudden booking offended her sense of order. How come the men had not known about it before, or had they simply forgotten to add it to the calendar? She didn't say anything though. Better pile a ziggurat of new books on her desk so that Simon couldn't ask her to do any extra jobs while the others were closeted in their office.

They had hoped that the Games would bring a bit of respite to the library team since several of the Trust's employees were away on holiday and others had volunteered to help with the Games. Unfortunately they found they had just as much work as before – in fact more, because Simon had been away at his conference and Crispin had been on holiday, so there was a lot of catching up to do. Quite the wrong time for two members of staff to have a teleconference for two hours, Simon thought. The cryptic note on the team calendar didn't even give him a clue as to which of the several TENNIS groups had arranged it. Why not phone the Senior Head of the TENNIS libraries, he thought; he could tell her about the conference while they were about it, including of course reporting on his successful paper. It was good to be a member of a network of libraries, in spite of occasional demands on the team to participate in working groups.

Simon forgot to ask about the teleconference once he started talking about the library conference, but his phone call was occasionally a little disturbed by the loud cheering from somewhere in the hospital. He turned round to see if any of the windows in his office were open, but they were all closed. He excused himself from the phone call for a moment and looked around the library lobby to check the windows there.

Sometimes in warm weather they could hear music from Slouch Ward below, or from the surrounding park. No doubt patients were listening to the Games now and cheering.

Eventually, Simon finished his phone call and crossed the lobby to ask if Lucy could photocopy a couple of documents for him. Just at that moment there was a loud cheer – in fact a veritable roar – and this time he knew exactly where it came from: Vlad and Crispin's office.

Contrary to all rules of politeness, Simon did not knock on the door, but flung it open without warning. There they were, Vladimir flailing his long arms victoriously and Crispin thumping him on the back, both of them half lying on top of Vlad's desk in front of the computer. Their cheer was echoed by the broadcast that they were watching.

Crispin turned round, his face flushed with excitement. "Guess what, Simon," he began. Then he realised that he was facing his boss, and his shoulders sank.

"Now then, you two," Simon said with a frown which Vlad recognised as the precursor to Expression 3B. "There is a twenty-metre shelf tidying event about to begin in the reading room. You two are the only participants."

With that, he turned round sharply and marched into the staff room, where he made a large pot of nice strong coffee, wondering when the next library journal would come out. It was sure to have a report of the library conference in it. If only they could have awarded gold medals for conference papers, he thought a little sadly.

THIRTY-SIX

A STITCH IN TIME

Simon opened the door to the Healthscare Library, his mind pleasantly on the new day ahead. Never mind such recent incidents as two of his staff spending time watching the Olympics when they should have been working; such minor problems were a part of the fabric of life and could be ironed out quickly by a skilful manager. The seamless operation of the library service had not been jeopardised.

The manager's good mood was instantly swept away by the scene that he saw unfolding in the library lobby. His heart raced for a few seconds, then missed a beat. The image of preparing for long jump flashed through his mind.

Claire Twinsett, his line manager, was standing in the middle of the lobby, and Lucy – the perfect, conscientious Lucy – was kneeling at Claire's feet. A tall, broad-shouldered man was standing with his back to the two women, but as soon as he turned round, Simon recognised Justin Drakonian. What on earth was the Chief Executive Officer doing in the library? It was unlikely that he wanted to join. The only possibility was that Lucy had done something horrible and was being disciplined not only by Simon's line manager, but by the CEO himself. More probably, she was exaggerating the effects of some trivial mistake and pleading for mercy. Or were Claire and Justin here to announce the dreaded relocation, and this was Lucy's response?

Somehow Simon managed to unfreeze himself and step forward, though he was sure the scene would be forever etched in his mind. Claire looked so disapproving – but then Claire usually did look disapproving. The expression of the CEO towering over the two women could not be interpreted. But he, Simon, was Lucy's line manager and therefore responsible for either defending or disciplining her. He therefore took three more steps, putting on a determined look.

But Lucy was the first to speak. "There you are, Claire," she said with a brisk movement of her hands, as if to snap a thread between them. Then she stood up.

"Thank you, Lucy," Claire replied, her disapproving look changing to something like approval-but-with-dignity.

"Well, I've never heard of repairing a hem being part of library services," the CEO boomed, his massive facial features rearranging themselves into a broad smile as he turned to Simon. "You've got an unusual team here," he continued, accepting a cup of tea which Vladimir was offering. Claire took hers with a condescending nod. Simon could only hope that his 'I'm glad to hear that' was uttered with the right tone even though he hadn't had time to pick up the thread yet.

After the visitors had left, Simon gradually unravelled the mystery. Claire had come in, but the hem of her skirt had become undone when it was caught in a splinter in the door. This of course was cause for concern and complaint on her part. A splinter was a Health and Safety issue, and what was it doing anyway in a door that had relatively recently been painted at great expense? Mimosa had therefore promised to fill in an incident report and was now pretending to be busy with it although she had no intention to fill one in really; the ever resourceful Lucy on her part had pulled out a sewing kit from her desk drawer and knelt down to stitch up Claire's hem. It was at that point that Justin Drakonian had chosen to drop in on his way to the corporate induction for new employees. Vladimir had hovered around for a while in the hope that he could ask the rare visitor to join the library, but Justin had evidently not even noticed him, watching the scene with such fascination, until Vlad had thought of offering both visitors a cup of tea. Crispin of course had missed the whole incident, because he was promoting the library services at the induction.

"You should still report the splinter to the Estates, Mimosa, even if you don't want to fill in an incident report about Claire's hem," Simon advised his assistant librarian when he realised that she had only been pretending about filling in the form.

"I know," was the surly reply. Why did Simon have to tell her what to do? She knew her job all right. It was bad enough having Claire come in and start barking at them, then the CEO who wouldn't even look into the reading room – their pride – or join the library. She didn't need Simon's advice; she only needed a coffee. She got up and went into the staff room to put the coffee on. This pleasurable activity made her feel better, and she began to reflect on the incident. She should have shown a more welcoming attitude to the visitors, and as for Simon, he had the right to advise her even if it was unnecessary in this case. She sighed and went back carrying two mugs, one for herself and one for her manager.

Meanwhile, Simon had recovered from his shock and was reflecting on his glorious ancestors. Who was it who according to family legend had had an incident etched in his mind? Wilhelm von Databerg? He was the one who had emigrated to Britain and been unable to communicate with his sweetheart except in Dewey Decimal until he learnt enough English. That was perhaps why his visual memory had been so keen that incidents etched themselves in his mind. Wilhelm had been a remarkable man, and it was a pity there was no Wikipedia entry about him. It was clearly Simon's duty to write one; he would just have to do a bit of research into family documents one of these days. Perhaps the entry could then be expanded to a full biography later on.

He turned to his emails, brushing aside all thoughts of Wilhelm and any other ancestors, as well as any thoughts of the morning's incident. After all, the team had behaved in an exemplary fashion. Ah, there was already an email from Claire; she must have sent it in response to the excellent and unusual service she had received.

'I know this is not a very important matter,' the email began, 'but perhaps I ought to point out that the cup of tea I was given in your library tasted as if it had been laced heavily with salt. It's worth bearing in mind in case you ever have to entertain Royal College inspectors or similar.'

Simon sighed. Who had made Claire's tea? In the scheme of things, was it important who the culprit was? But he made a mental note to mention it to his staff. It couldn't have been an accident – the only salt they kept in the cupboard was in tiny paper sachets such as you were given with your lunch tray on flights (he himself had brought back a few from his trip to the library conference), whereas their sugar was stored in its original bag.

He opened the next email. Children's Services team at Knowl Edge? Interesting – they rarely used the library services because of their remote location, which was why one of Crispin's tasks was to promote electronic access and the option of having books sent in the internal mail.

'We're writing to thank the Healthscare Library for the generous gift of one thousand packs of gummed and assorted paper strips for making paper chains. We've already made little sets of Olympic rings, and soon we'll be turning our minds to suitable crafts for Christmas,' Simon read. His head reeled. One thousand packs of paper strips donated by his library? There must be a mistake somewhere. But the message went on to say that Vladimir had delivered them in person. Had his staff got together behind his back and decided to make a donation to the Children's Services? But in that case, why leave him out of such a generous act?

There could be another explanation, but he didn't feel strong enough to check the financial accounts for any unusual activity without another cup of coffee. Getting up, Simon swore to himself that this was the last time he would leave the library to go to conferences, on annual leave, Bank Holidays, or on sick leave. By Jove, he would chain himself to his desk. He had a momentary vision of his wife phoning and pleading with him to come home, then of Claire marching in and threatening him with disciplinary action. But never mind, he would persist. Perhaps one could order a length of sturdy chain from NHS Cargo?

THIRTY-SEVEN

EVERY GOOD LIBRARY HAS ONE

There was a tiny voice that said clearly and with evident satisfaction: *Copy. Pate. Copy. Pate.* Mimosa thought at first that she was dreaming of teaching computer literacy. Then she realised she was awake and that the voice belonged to Emily, who had come into the bedroom and was climbing into her mother's bed.

Through a crack in the curtains Mimosa saw that the moon was nearly full. She sighed; Emily was always restless at full moon and tended to wake up in the middle of the night or else far too early for Mimosa's liking, and usually couldn't be settled again.

"Copy. Pate." The voice was close to Mimosa's head now. Really, she said to herself, Grandpa should stop trying to teach computer skills to such a young child. Then she felt something on her hair and passed a hand through it. It was sticky and smelt of peppermint. "Pate!" Emily announced with glee and held up a tube of toothpaste for her mother to see in the moonlight. Then, with a determined "Cut!" she slid off the bed and headed towards the place where the forbidden scissors lived. Mimosa decided with resignation that it was time to get up and see what highlights made with toothpaste looked like.

***

When she finally arrived at work, Mimosa had to face a complaint. Two nursing students had stayed on late in the library the night before and swore that they had heard a ghost, which they said was unacceptable and the librarians should do something about it. She promised they would investigate, though she had no intention of doing so. She would have simply ignored such a silly thing, had Lucy not overheard the conversation and brought it up in the team meeting later on that day.

The rest of the team showed great interest in the ghost. Vladimir announced that every good library had a ghost, particularly in an old building such as theirs, and that he had secretly wished for years that they had one. Simon wanted to interrogate the students; he was suspicious because they claimed that they had heard a ghost but not seen it. Lucy didn't want to have anything to do with any ghosts, seen or unseen. Mimosa pointed out that since ghosts didn't exist, it didn't matter whether the students claimed their experience had been visual or auditory. Crispin only opened his mouth to yawn.

"You wouldn't talk like that if you heard a ghost yourself," Vlad said and let out an unearthly howl to demonstrate. Two startled library users looked in to see what was going on in the staff room. "That's what a ghost sounds like," Vlad stated with conviction.

"Rubbish!" Mimosa said. "Prove it!" She shouldn't have said that, because as soon as the team meeting was over, Vlad spent an hour doing a literature search to find evidence of the sound that ghosts traditionally were believed to make. In the end, he had to admit that the evidence wasn't there and that in any case he had never actually heard a ghost himself.

When the two students came back, Mimosa asked them about the ghost again. What exactly had they heard, and where?

"Footsteps," Hector said, lowering his voice. "Steady, marching footsteps. We were upstairs in the stacks looking for an old edition of a nursing textbook. But when we looked out of the window, we couldn't see anybody." He cast a glance at Mimosa. Was the assistant librarian ageing prematurely, or were those white streaks in her hair highlights?

Mimosa promised they would talk to Security. It was a good job they had at last a security man on site again, after there had been two attempted burglaries on the premises. No doubt Security could put an end to this nonsense.

But the same thing was repeated the following night, and the night after; the students had stayed late in the library and had heard footsteps upstairs. Simon contacted Security. He contacted Reception. He contacted Estates and Facilities. No one had heard or seen anything out of the ordinary. In the end, Simon even contacted Simon Spindrift, the most senior of all Senior Nurses, an expert on the history of the hospital. But there was nothing in the history of the hospital to suggest any paranormal activity.

"We'll mount a watch," Simon declared to his team. "We'll take turns staying in the library after hours. I suggest two of us each night. Any volunteers to start off?"

Mimosa would have been willing in principle, provided she was allowed to catch up with her work at the same time, but she didn't want to impose on her mother to look after Emily at night, and Simon pointed out that it would be difficult for her to do her cataloguing or book ordering while upstairs in the stacks. Lucy was afraid but didn't want to say so, though her reluctance was obvious to everyone. Crispin didn't want to trouble himself but didn't want to say so; instead, he promised to consider the matter, provided he could have the following day off. Vladimir reminded Simon that working unsocial hours would mean being paid at a higher rate, and said he hoped the library budget was up to it.

In the end, Simon said he would take on the first night himself. As it happened, Dr Terremoto, who had heard about the ghost from the students, had already expressed his willingness to join any investigation as he was on call anyway. Mimosa bit her lip, wishing she could have changed her mind and taken Simon's place.

It was a cold night, but Massimo Terremoto was prepared and was wearing a thick sweater. Simon felt cold, but was determined not to let it show because his companion might think he was shivering with fright. They had agreed they would try to make do with natural light in the stacks in case anything suspicious – whether a burglar or a ghost – turned up and might have been scared away by electric lights. Luckily the moon was full and there were no clouds.

After two hours of idle sitting around in the stacks and making desultory conversation in a low voice, Dr Terremoto suddenly stopped and cocked his head to listen. "That was an owl," he said. "It did sound eerie! I didn't know there were any owls here in the hospital grounds. But it must have been somewhere quite far."

Simon thought it was more likely to have been the bird clock in his office, and the owl meant that it was midnight. They decided it was time for a hot drink, and Simon therefore got up and went downstairs to make one for both of them. He brought two mugs of tea to the bay window where Dr Terremoto was seated and put them down on the small table that they had pulled up for the purpose. He was about to say something when the doctor suddenly held out his hand in a warning gesture. Then Simon heard it, too: footsteps. Steady but soft footsteps, approaching from the left.

The men stood up and moved to the window without a sound. As if by agreement, they each stood half covered by a curtain so that they could look down without being visible themselves. But nothing could be seen; only the soft footsteps could be heard through the closed single glazing as they passed slowly but steadily under the window.

Simon realised that they hadn't made a plan for this. What should they do now? Challenge the, erm, ghost? A burglar would in all likelihood run away, unless he had a gun and was in a violent and desperate mood. Anyone simply wanting to take a walk was unlikely to do so in the hospital grounds at midnight immediately under the windows. A ghost? Would a ghost move with audible footsteps? What was a ghost by definition, anyway? Vlad's literature search had been a waste of time.

The footsteps stopped under the window. Simon felt a crawling, cold sensation in the nape of his neck. What if it was... Then he smelt smoke. Dr Terremoto must have noticed it at the same moment, because he made a gesture as if sniffing the air. He opened the window very slowly, and by good fortune it was one that didn't creak. He leaned out as far as he could in order to gain a view over the window ledge, then retreated almost violently, turning to Simon with a look of anger on his face.

"Security man," he mouthed and mimed the action of smoking a cigarette. Simon couldn't understand why the doctor looked so angry – all right, smoking was forbidden on the premises – but then he remembered that Dr Terremoto was one of the hospital's smoking cessation champions. They moved away from the window and had a quick whispered discussion about the best course of action. It didn't take long, and both men nodded and smiled broadly. Simon went to one of the shelves, pulled out a book and tiptoed to the window. He leaned out exactly where a thin wisp of smoke could be seen rising up, took aim, and dropped the book on the man's head. A grunt and a swearword could be heard; after that, the footsteps resumed again, but this time much faster and receding rapidly into the distance.

Simon closed the window and picked up his tea.

"Cheers, Massimo," he said smiling and raising his mug to his companion. "I'm glad that book on smoking cessation found its target audience at last."

THIRTY-EIGHT

CRISPIN'S FAN CLUB

The weather was hot, there was no doubt about it. Even the worst pessimists and moaners had to admit that it *was* hot and sunny (as it ought to be in the summertime), but the worst moaners soon found reason to moan because it was too hot to work.

The Healthscare Library stayed nice and cool for a few days longer than most places because it was in an old building with thick stone walls. Moreover, because the library wasn't like the inpatient areas that had to be kept warm and therefore ventilated with due caution, one could open the windows any time. Only on a crack due to pigeon chains, mind you, but even that let in some cool air. But eventually the heat penetrated the library, especially the reading room, which was south facing and had plenty of large windows. No amount of tomato plants could have shaded it sufficiently, and it would have been nice if one could have pushed the windows wide open.

The Trust dress code stated exactly what employees were allowed to wear, and in particular what they were *not* allowed to wear, to wit shorts, sleeveless tops, or miniskirts; anything that would have made the employees feel a bit cooler. Mimosa was furious because so much of it seemed to be directed towards women, at least by implication. But Vlad was quick to point out that Justin Drakonian the CEO was no more entitled to wear shorts than she, Mimosa.

"We've got to do something," Lucy said after the second reader had been ushered out in a state of near heatstroke.

"Let's rip the pigeon chains off," Vlad suggested, rubbing his hands together. He was itching for some action again.

"We'll do no such thing," Simon said firmly. "The solution is quite simple, and I'm amazed that none of you have thought of it yet: we must buy a pedestal fan. Lucy, you order one from S-Cargo as a matter of urgency, please."

Setting to work, Lucy spent the next half hour trying to identify a pedestal fan in the catalogue. She struggled through entries such as *Pedestal – mats. Pedestal – toilets. Ventilation unit: see Fan. Fan: see Ventilation unit.* At last she found what she wanted and created the order online. It was duly authorised by Simon, but was of course returned immediately with a query from the Supplies team as to a clinical need to have a pedestal fan in the library. It only took a phone call from Simon to sort out the matter, since he was able to provide the names of the two readers who had had to be removed from the now tropical reading room. He was still annoyed that he had had to fill in a time-consuming incident report about it, but at least it meant he had the names to hand. However, the cost of the fan was so high that Simon wondered if it was best not to test the stretching capacity of his budget after all.

"What if Claire demands that we return the fan when she hears about it?" he said to Mimosa, whose opinion he was seeking on the matter.

"In that case Claire can come and stand in the reading room and fan library users nine till five. Outside hours, they'll have to faint," Mimosa suggested calmly.

Simon cast a sideways glance at his assistant librarian, wondering for a moment whether to reprimand her for such callousness. Then he decided to let the remark pass and got up instead, announcing that he was going to town on business.

He returned carrying a large and unwieldy parcel. It contained a pedestal fan, which to everybody's delight had cost far less than an S-Cargo one; besides, it was there *now* rather than a week later. The only snag was how Simon was going to be reimbursed since the Cashier's office did not allow petty cash to be taken out.

"Never mind, we can start putting our photocopying money aside unless people ask for a receipt," he said. "That way it shouldn't take long till we've got the sum together."

"By the time we've got the sum together, your receipt will have faded out of all recognition or you will have retired, whichever comes first," Vladimir predicted. Simon cast a disapproving glance at him and started to unpack the fan. Crispin, who was supposed to write up his statistics on last quarter's outreach activities but didn't feel like it, volunteered to help.

The fan was set up quickly and it worked. Two readers who had been wilting at their computers immediately revived, one of them to complain that the fan created a draught, the other one to remark that it was rather noisy. But when Simon switched the fan off and threatened to transfer it into the staff room, it suddenly became a highly desirable object.

And so all was well for a few days. To be precise, all was well from Friday afternoon when the fan was purchased, until Monday morning when the library staff returned after the weekend and found the fan gone. They spent a good twenty minutes interrogating each other about it, but to no avail. None of them had moved it accidentally, wilfully, or absentmindedly.

The heatwave continued. Lucy put up notices asking for news of the missing object. She put up several in the library, one in the ladies' toilet – Vlad put another one in the gents' – and would have taken one to the staff canteen, but Simon stopped her in case Claire saw it.

"Come on, boss, you've done nothing wrong," Mimosa said impatiently. "You've bought a fan and that's it, all for the sake of our precious users. If anybody has done something wrong, it's the thief."

Of course they mentioned the fan to Adonis, who promised to keep his eyes open in the section of the hospital that he was responsible for. He also promised to alert the other cleaners, though it was unlikely that the fan would have been carried very far.

The following morning a doctor reported a fan had turned up in his ward, but when Lucy went there to investigate, it was the wrong fan. She returned completely downcast because she had found the experience so embarrassing.

"Come on, Lucy, I'm sure you did nothing wrong," Mimosa said impatiently. "You know how to handle these situations. I mean, surely you didn't just blurt out 'That must be our stolen fan,' or something?" But Lucy swore that from now on she would leave all investigations to her colleagues.

Mimosa left Lucy to deal with her rebuff as best she could, and went downstairs to buy a sandwich. She stood in the queue behind the ward manager of Slouch Ward and decided to strike up a conversation. Of course it started with a reference to the unusual weather, both herself and Sam Snake agreeing that it was becoming unbearable. But when Mimosa mentioned their short-lived pedestal fan, Sam frowned and said rather curtly that he had no knowledge of such an object.

Adonis came back with news the same afternoon, soon after Mimosa's chat with Sam Snake. The cleaner told them with great excitement that he had overheard Sam say to one of his nurses that the library fan was now in the TV room of the ward. Adonis could quote him verbatim: "They'll never find it there," the ward manager had said to his colleague.

A heated discussion followed in the library staff room, during which Vlad nearly knocked over the coffee pot and Lucy nearly burst into tears twice. "We can't do anything," Simon said for the hundredth time. "You can't just march into Slouch Ward and..." "Can't we just?" challenged Crispin and got up so quickly that he knocked the biscuit tin flying. Before Simon had time to stop Crispin, he had slipped out of the room.

Vlad grabbed Simon by the arm when he tried to follow. "Let Cris do a bit of outreach," he said with a grin. It suited him better than a smile, Mimosa thought.

Crispin ran down the stairs and into the corridor where Slouch Ward was. At the entrance he saw Sam Snake, whose expression changed into alarm when he saw the librarian.

"I've come to pick up our fan," Crispin said. Before the ward manager had had time to draw breath, Crispin had already got into the TV room. It was full of patients, sitting or half-lying, some of them watching TV or chatting to each other. One or two were dozing. The room was very comfortable with the pedestal fan spreading coolness, and Crispin felt a moment's pity towards the patients. But the fan belonged to the library and had been purchased by the library, so Slouch Ward could do the same thing if only Sam got his act together.

Crispin moved deftly between chairs, saying lightly but very audibly: "Excuse me, I'll just pick up this fan and take it to where it belongs." Then the air current stopped, the fan was no longer there, and in two seconds the visitor was gone.

He got back to the library slightly out of breath, having carried the heavy fan up the stairs while keeping up his speed in case Sam followed. A fresh pot of coffee was made immediately to celebrate the Return of the Fan. While it was brewing, three readers stood to attention at the door of the reading room, equally pleased with the recovery of the lost object. It was plugged in and switched on again, and the readers cheered.

Lucy, full of remorse, pointed out to her colleagues that she had never labelled the fan and therefore Sam had been able to take it.

"Sam could have taken the fan even if you'd plastered it with ownership labels," Mimosa said a little impatiently. "It's just that it might have been found more quickly if you'd labelled it. There's a permanent marker, use that – who knows but somebody might try and scratch off a label. Somebody removed a barcode from one of the books last week."

The next day, an envelope arrived in the library anonymously with an ultraviolet marker in it. They never found out who had sent it, though Mimosa suspected Sam Snake. In any case the fan had already been marked clearly, and at the weekend the weather changed to torrential rain.

THIRTY-NINE

A CHANGE IS AS GOOD AS A REST

Simon pushed his chair back. "Leave your book list with me and I'll take care of it. Now go home and pack, and have a good holiday," he said to Mimosa. They had been spending the last twenty minutes of the day going through those of Mimosa's tasks that could not wait until her return from annual leave. What caused her most concern was that she was behind schedule on book purchases and didn't want to find herself with too much money at the end of the financial year. Somehow she hadn't found the time to put in an order before going away, and she was now kicking herself for not prioritising her tasks differently. Simon had reminded her that they were still nearer to the beginning than the end of the year, and secondly she could leave her book suggestions with him. She agreed a little reluctantly, admitting that what Simon said made sense.

Mimosa had often had arguments with her manager because she didn't take her annual leave as she should. Her excuse was always that too many things piled up in her absence. No one took up her cataloguing and acquisitions duties, and obviously no one checked her emails – the only things that got done were the routine jobs that they all took turns with anyway, such as staffing the enquiry desk. Simon always pointed out that this was the case with the rest of them, except with the library assistant since her tasks had to be carried out on a daily basis and thus the others had to deal with them in Lucy's absence. But now he had decided it was time to do things differently, and they could experiment by taking care of some of Mimosa's tasks. The word 'experiment' caused such a look of horror on her face that Simon had to change it quickly to something less adventurous before going into details.

The assistant librarian had thus gone on her holiday, but the library manager's thoughts of development did not stop there. Why should he handle Mimosa's book order? Lucy could do it since all that was needed was creating the order online on the NHS Cargo website and then having somebody else authorise it. Or – better still – Mimosa's original list could wait till her return, since she seemed so nervous about leaving it to the others. This was an excellent opportunity to rotate their tasks, so why not go a step further and allow Crispin and Vladimir to select some titles? They could then create the order on S-Cargo rather than leave it to Lucy, and that way they would see the whole procedure from beginning to end.

A little to Simon's surprise, Vlad and Crispin were delighted with his idea. They didn't usually agree so readily to any extra work. Perhaps it was the novelty of it; that was worth bearing in mind. A good library manager should always think of ways of re-energising his staff and developing their skills, Simon said to himself. Then he collected his papers and set off to a meeting at Cardiack Hill, where Dr Achinside had promised to give him a lift as his own car was at the garage.

Vlad and Crispin set to work as soon as the library door had closed behind the manager. They started by looking up the section on acquisitions in the Policy and Procedures folder, which contained all that was necessary to know about the working of the Healthscare Library. "Boring," was Crispin's verdict. "It's all about how you select the titles according to what areas the users are likely to want. And then you have to follow minute little details of creating the order on S-Cargo."

"Easy," Vlad countered. "Lucy can create the order, it's a routine task and we need not worry about it, whatever Simon says. We simply give her our list of books, and I'll authorise the order."

"But what about selecting the books?" Crispin insisted, throwing the folder on his desk. "How on earth do we know what our users want? We've got all kinds of clinical staff and admin people and students, so it's going to take for ever to select something for everybody."

"You're right there, and that's what we'll do: select something for everybody. But we'll do it our way," Vlad said triumphantly. "Mimosa and the boss will be impressed!"

He picked up the folder. "First we must check how much money there is left in the book budget," he said a little self-importantly. Cris clearly hadn't thought of this, but he, Vladimir, was not the deputy manager for nothing. "Ah, I've found the place where it tells you how to check that," he said. "Let's get down to work."

It didn't take them long to spot something interesting on the bookseller's website that suited the budget. "There are two editions, but this is the one we want," Crispin said, pointing to an entry on the screen. "You want a good, sturdy edition, something to last a lifetime."

"Agreed," Vlad said with a grin and wrote down the details on his notepad. "De luxe. What else shall we buy?"

Having finished their selection, they handed the notepad to Lucy for creating the order. But somehow the job didn't seem completed: they felt they ought to withdraw a corresponding amount of books to make space for the new ones. They took a tape measure and went into the reading room. "First in, first out," Crispin said. "That's the principle, isn't it?" He headed for the corner where the historical collection was housed. With a look of satisfaction, he rolled up his sleeves.

Lucy protested a little when she was presented with an armful of eighteenth and nineteenth century volumes to withdraw, but her fiancé was adamant. "Just do the usual stuff," he said. "Cross out the barcodes, clap on 'withdrawn' stamps, and whatever you normally have to do with old books."

"It's all in Policy and Procedures," Crispin added, but Lucy had one of her rare moments when the worm turned, and she told him that he could teach his grandmother to suck eggs. In her mind, she wondered who would see to it that the books were also withdrawn from the catalogue; usually it was Mimosa's job. Perhaps she should pile the books on Simon's desk after finishing her bit so that he could amend the catalogue entries.

When Simon returned from his meeting at Cardiack Hill, the two men were already waiting for him impatiently, their faces glowing with pride. They said they had made their selection and Lucy had created the order on S-Cargo.

"Impressive," the manager said. "I'm really pleased. Have you got a print-out of the order? I'd like to see what you've purchased." It wasn't really important that they hadn't entered the order on S-Cargo themselves, the main thing in this case was the decision process. He shifted aside two piles of books from the historical collection, which for some reason had been parked on his desk.

"There's one little snag," Vlad said, looking embarrassed all of a sudden. He held back the sheet of paper that contained the order, which Simon was reaching to take from his hand. "Maybe you'll understand if you look at the order online. There seems to be a problem."

Simon unlocked his PC and logged into the NHS Cargo website. There was a message for him regarding an order that had been created and authorised that morning. Drat it, what was the problem then? Had S-Cargo messed things up again, or was it the Finance department this time? There couldn't be a financial problem, because Vlad as deputy manager could authorise orders up to—

Simon let his hands sink into his lap. The order itself was simple enough as it consisted of two items only. It was the message in red that drew his attention. It stated that the Healthscare Library's book budget had been overdrawn and the matter had been referred to Claire Twinsett. Simon didn't understand this at all. Mimosa couldn't possibly have spent so much since she had said herself that she was behind schedule with book orders. Had she made a huge mistake, so that just two more items had exceeded the budget? Or... what exactly were those two items that had been ordered? He turned and snatched the order sheet from Vlad's hand.

"We thought it would be clever to use up the remaining budget," Crispin said. "That will save Mimosa no end of work."

"No more acquisitions to do until next financial year," Vladimir echoed. Why was Simon looking so pale? Wasn't he feeling very well?

Simon looked up from the print-out he had been staring at in disbelief. "Um, I'd like to hear how you selected just these two particular items," he said as calmly as he could. His ancestors would have been proud of him, he thought.

"Easy," Vlad said shrugging his shoulders. "*Encyclopaedia Britannica*, something to suit everybody, and a sturdy leather-backed edition to take any amount of handling by the punters. It said on the bookshop website we would get a really good discount. Then the paperback on appendix operations because we had a bit of money left over."

"And *How to Take out Your Own Appendix* is suitable for everybody because it's a self-help book," Crispin continued. Surely the boss couldn't have anything against that?

"And then we withdrew a lot of old books to make space for the Britannica," Vlad added, pointing to the books piled on the desk.

Simon opened one of them. A large, black stamp saying WITHDRAWN was neatly (and indelibly) placed across Samuel Johnson's signature on the flyleaf. Simon thought it was better to deal with one problem at a time, so he drew a deep breath and explained that the bookseller's website didn't offer 'really good discounts' to the NHS but only to online customers of the bookshop. It was an understandable error. The question was now how he would explain the overspend –

a hefty one – to his line manager, as Claire could be difficult at the best of times.

As if reading his thoughts, the phone rang. It was Claire, wishing to discuss the library's book budget.

"Hold the line a moment, please," Simon said suavely and then covered the receiver. "Vlad, I know you've always wanted to practise your skills as library manager," he said. "I've just remembered I left my headlights on. You take this call while I nip down to the car."

He thrust the receiver into Vlad's hand and ran for it. Crispin cast a long and puzzled look after him. How could Simon have left his headlights on, when he had told them earlier that his car was at the garage?

FORTY

THINGS FALL APART

Vladimir stormed into the library. No one had ever seen him in such a foul mood; he could be impatient, indignant, irritated, but now he looked as if he could express himself in expletives and even become downright explosive.

"So much for my training session for the junior doctors," he announced as soon as he spotted Simon. "Please excuse me from any further training sessions – individual *or* group. Samosa can do them, or Cris. Or you."

The injured trainer disappeared into his office and slammed the door behind him so that it made Simon jump. He felt a twinge of jealousy: hadn't he recently tried to slam his door in anger but hadn't succeeded because it closed too softly? Maybe he could ask Al Monte to come and examine the two doors. Do a comparative study.

Simon roused himself. Something very bad must have happened to make Vlad behave like that, and it was his line manager's duty to find out what it was. He went into the staff room, filled a mug with coffee, knocked on Vlad's door, opened it a crack, and pushed the mug through it just so far that it could be seen. A hand appeared and snatched it, but it was not the long-fingered hand Simon had expected, but a fleshy paw covered with sand-coloured curly hair.

"No, Crispin!" he shouted, but it was too late – he had let go of the mug. He barely managed to pull his hand away before the door closed again. He could hear Crispin's voice calling out "Thanks, boss!" with evident satisfaction. Simon sighed and turned away, only to be faced with a dissatisfied assistant librarian. "This place will fall to pieces one day," Mimosa said crossly.

"So it will, if those men keep slamming the door," Simon retorted. He didn't want to hear any more complaints today. He wanted a nice, quiet library with contented, well-behaved colleagues and contented, well-behaved customers. And if the library was moved to some other location in the near future, it didn't really matter whether this place fell to pieces or not.

Mimosa ignored his comment and proceeded to explain. The Trust had recently installed new style soap dispensers in the toilets. Simon nodded; he had noticed them. There were no instructions on how to use them, but he had managed to work out a satisfactory way of extracting one small drop of liquid soap at a time. This was evidently a daily allowance. Now Mimosa told him that the dispenser in the ladies' toilet near the library had been broken for weeks, probably because the ladies had manhandled it.

Here Simon had to reprimand Mimosa for her language. "All right, person-handled then," she continued. She had finally reported the broken dispenser to Facilities. Simon nodded approvingly: so she should have done. The next day, the dispenser appeared to have been replaced as there was a large amount of escaped soap all over the wall and the hand basin. Mimosa recognised the replacement as the old model, so therefore she concluded it must in fact be an old one, taken from another toilet in all probability. Her suspicion was soon proved correct because the dispenser kept falling apart. Mimosa then buttonholed Al Monte from the Estates when she saw him in the canteen. Poor Al confessed he had taken the dispenser out of the gents, and Crispin – who had been sent to reconnoitre – reported back to Mimosa that their dispenser had indeed walked.

"I'm not sure if I've followed this thread," Simon admitted. "What exactly do you want me to do? I'm a library manager, not a—"

Mimosa looked fiercely at her boss. "And I'm an assistant librarian, and I've got other things to do besides complaining about Health and Safety issues. But if no one else cares, then fine, somebody must take responsibility. Did you know that in the last Trust staff survey, six percent of the respondents claimed they didn't know whether paper towels and soap were always available? Don't those people ever want to wash their hands properly?"

Simon looked perplexed. "Perhaps they were being honest," he suggested. "Perhaps they didn't know whether paper towels and soap were *always* available?"

There was the shrill sound of the doorbell. Lucy answered it and came into the lobby to say that the lightning conductor man was on his way to the library.

The library manager's jaw dropped. His dentist would have found it easy to work there.

"Lightning conductor? I didn't know we had one," he said feebly. Mimosa told him that there was one on the roof, only accessible from the stacks, and the Estates manager had told her it was due for an inspection. The library therefore was responsible for letting the technician in when he arrived.

Simon was relieved to have Mimosa's attention directed away from the matter of hand washing. His staff were behaving very oddly today; it could have been straight out of a soap opera. The root of the problem was, he thought, that Mimosa tended to reflect too much and Vlad too little.

A wizened man in a faded blue jacket limped in. "This must be the library," he said. "You had something wrong with your lightning conductor, I hear." His jacket sported the logo of a company, but Mimosa couldn't read the name as it was almost worn off. She offered to show the man upstairs.

"What a lot of stairs," the man commented as he followed her. "I'm not very good with stairs any longer, you know." He was beginning to develop a slight wheeze, but made it to the upper floor without collapsing. They wound their way through the shelves to the side window. Mimosa unlatched it with some difficulty and pushed it as far open as she could. It was a good thing the man was quite small; a larger man wouldn't have been able to squeeze through. She reached out and pointed to the lightning conductor, which could be seen on the roof top and apparently very near to falling off it, judging by the way it was swaying in the wind.

"Oh no, sweetheart, I couldn't possibly get up *there*," the man said. "Me old knees wouldn't let me. Besides, I haven't got any ropes with me, nor a ladder either. You'll have to call somebody else. Health and Safety, you know." Mimosa ground her teeth and explained to the man that it wasn't her job to call in lightning conductor inspectors. It was simply that their roof happened to be the place where the thing was located, and Mr Moore-Gubbins had asked them to help with access.

She led the man downstairs again and was relieved to have her attention directed away from lightning conductors by a porter who entered manoeuvring a wire cage on wheels. He pushed it right to the middle of the lobby and stopped in front of Vlad and Crispin's office. The cage was stacked with cardboard boxes, all alike.

Mimosa looked questioningly at Lucy, who looked questioningly at Simon. He shrugged his shoulders and turned to the porter. They had never seen the man before – must be new, or a temp – but they could recognise him as a porter from the T-shirt that bore the Trust logo. Rogues rarely came bearing gifts, Simon thought, so this must be a genuine porter. Or could it be that the boxes were empty, and while they were examining them, the man would sneak into the office and rifle the cash tin... He had already started unloading the boxes, which all had the name of a computer company on them. They did seem to contain something judging by the way the man was handling them.

Lucy was the first to speak. "I don't think we've ordered anything recently," she said. "At least not PCs. At least not so many." She sent another questioning glance in Simon's direction.

At that moment, Vladimir finally emerged from his office. Or rather, he would have emerged, had the cage not been standing right in front of the door. It looked as if he himself was in a cage, peering through the wire. Mimosa frowned: the porter should have found a better place to park that cage – not in front of somebody's office. Health and Safety, she said to herself.

"It says here I've got to deliver eleven computers," the man said, interrupting his work and waving a crumpled piece of paper in Lucy's direction. Vlad let out a roar.

"Don't talk to me about computers!" he shouted and shook the cage by its frame.

"No one was talking to you!" Mimosa snapped. "What's wrong with you today?"

The porter turned back and started piling more boxes on the floor. Funny people, librarians, he thought. They sounded just as if they were rehearsing a family drama. Maybe they *were* doing a drama? Candid camera or something? He glanced round to see if there was a CCTV anywhere to be seen, and smiled quickly at everyone in case a hidden camera had focused on him.

"I don't want to see any computers," Vlad bellowed, still holding on to the cage. Then he seemed to calm down a little. "Not here at any rate. I went into the IT training room this morning to deliver a training session—"

He paused for a moment. Simon nodded: so he should have done; that was what had been scheduled. *Yearn to Learn*, the session was called.

"But there were no computers," Vlad completed his sentence. "Not a single one. They'd all been removed without prior warning. And the doctors all thought it was our fault and that we'd messed up our training schedule."

The phone started ringing in the office and Lucy ran to pick it up. It was John Upskill from the Learning department, wishing to speak to Vladimir.

Before anyone else had time to move, Simon was in the office. "Hello, John, this is Simon," he said. "I'm afraid Vladimir is not available right now." He glanced across the

231

lobby, where Vlad was trying to push the cage away from the doorway but the pile of boxes on the other side was obstructing it. "A delivery of PCs? Yes, we have them here in the library. Somewhat unexpected, I would say... An upgrade for the IT training room? To replace the ones that were removed without prior warning?"

"Yes, but what about rescheduling Vlad's training session?" Expression 3B was clearly creeping into Simon's voice as he spoke up for his injured, indignant, but slightly infantile IT trainer.

At that moment there was a tremendous crash from the lobby. A stack of eleven computer boxes had toppled over as Vlad had finally managed to shift the crate that had blocked his way. The porter cast one look at the tall man wading through the boxes and striding into the office where the telephone conversation was still going on.

"I've had enough," the porter announced. "I'm washing my hands of this." He turned and walked out, leaving the empty cage behind. Who wanted libraries, anyway? Nowadays you could find everything on the internet.

FORTY-ONE

PARKING PROBLEMS AT BACKWATER

The taller of the two policemen bent down to hear better what the little old lady was telling him. It seemed that she had got lost and couldn't find her daughter's car again in the busy car park of Backwater Health Centre. Her daughter had dropped her off and told her to enjoy herself; it was the day of the annual Backwater Rowing and Sewing event for staff, patients and their families. They were to have met there again in an hour's time, which would be very soon now, but the old lady had little idea what make her daughter's car was and still less the registration number. All she could say was that it was a small, red car.

"Does your daughter have a mobile phone we could ring?" the policeman asked. But the old lady couldn't remember the number and didn't have it with her. In the end, one of the policemen offered to escort her to the coffee stall so she could sit down while the other one would go and ask the organisers to make a public announcement.

On the other side of the car park, Crispin Curlewe was approaching the health centre in his car. The road leading there was blocked almost completely by cars waiting to drive in, an hour after the event had started. Crispin estimated it would take several minutes before he could even dream of moving on. His bag was lying on the passenger seat, and he pulled it closer and began to examine the contents for something with which to pass the time. Ah yes, here it was. He had come to the conclusion a long time ago that the surest way to keep calm was to have something interesting but relaxing to do while waiting.

Marvellous how this event was drawing people. He had expected at least the road to be clear so he could drive straight in, and of course there would be a problem with parking, once he had got as far as the car park. His library promotion – which Simon had insisted on calling *Row, Sew and Know* – was not scheduled to start until eleven o'clock, but it was always nice to be there on time. It was a good way to save one's nerves, and also a good way to avoid complaints; Crispin still remembered his first promotional event, which had ended before it had even started.

At last the queue in front of Crispin began to move. With his bag on his knee, he released the handbrake, then let the car roll forwards very slowly. Would he find somewhere to park? Worst case scenario, he would have to turn back and report to Simon that he hadn't been able to do the promo because of parking problems. Perhaps he could take a photo of the sea of cars as evidence?

He coasted the car park and, miraculously, somebody pulled out just in front of him. He waited until he could slip in, then parked, took his promotional materials out of the bag and got out briskly. He threw the bag on the driver's seat, remembering briefly the warning that one should never leave any bags where they could be spotted by thieves. But it was getting late, and he would still have to find the room where his promo was going to be.

The two policemen had met outside the coffee stall again and started walking slowly and methodically round the car park. The little old lady was safe where she was – enjoying a cup of tea at the stall – and apparently not too worried about meeting her daughter; she had heard the announcement as it came out of the rattling loudspeakers, and she had every faith in the nice officers who had helped her. Her only chagrin was that she hadn't brought her knitting to pass the time, she said. As for the daughter, she would now know that her elderly mother was safe, and would know where to find her. So, patrolling the car park would be a good thing for the policemen to do at this point as it was becoming clear that the day would break all records in the brief history of the Backwater Rowing and Sewing event. And in a busy place there were always things the police had to watch out for: car thieves (there had been a couple of attempted break-ins at Backwater recently), pickpockets, small accidents when people backed their cars and didn't look what they were doing; and lost little old ladies.

The shorter of the two policemen stopped suddenly. There was a small red car standing at the edge of the car park, and as they approached, they saw there was a bag lying on the driver's seat with a ball of wool that had fallen out. The tip of something sharp, evidently a knitting needle, was sticking out slightly.

"I think we've got it," the taller man said with satisfaction. "I'll take down the number just in case. You go and tell the old lady."

A little later, Crispin emerged from the hospital building. His presentation had aroused quite a lot of interest in the audience – mainly nurses and students on placement – and he had managed to fit in some jokes about teaching them the Know but not the Row and Sew. Most people had picked up a library membership form and some of his leaflets; in fact by the end of the short promo slot, everything that Lucy had produced for the event had gone. The forms, once filled in, would be returned to the library in the internal mail.

Crispin slowed down his steps. Was there something he had forgotten? Hadn't he had a plastic wallet for the papers? He looked round to see if he had dropped it in the car park, but couldn't see it. He had reached his car before he remembered that he hadn't had any plastic wallet, only the papers he had pulled out of his bag. He hesitated once more, a little puzzled about this lapse of memory, and looked round again before feeling his pockets for the keys.

The taller policeman nudged his colleague. They had been walking back from the coffee stall – where the old lady was still happily sitting and waiting for her daughter – and had noticed the man with curly hair who had suddenly began to walk more slowly and look around. Now he had stopped by the old lady's daughter's car and was hesitating, looking round once more... The story didn't tally: the old lady had definitely said daughter, not son, and even though she had been a little scatty, this was a point that she couldn't possibly have been wrong about. Here was a car thief, and he would be caught red-handed!

Crispin swung round when the policemen spoke to him. They wanted to see his papers.

"I'm sorry, I haven't got any papers now," he explained. "I gave them all away at the event."

The men looked at each other. This was developing into an interesting day: a lost old lady and a car thief who claimed he had given his papers away. Must be having a sudden identity crisis, one of the men said to himself with a wry smile, making a mental note to comment to his colleague afterwards.

"You mean you gave your ID away at the event?" he asked, stepping closer. Crispin gave a little laugh and got out his driving license. "Sorry, I misunderstood you," he said. "I've just been doing a library promotion, and I thought you meant the leaflets. I was wondering why you wanted to join an NHS library!"

Hmm... an unusual excuse. The policemen glanced at each other again. Then they asked the inevitable question: was this his car?

Crispin was beginning to feel nervous. Why on earth were they interrogating him? He pulled out the car keys and opened the door. "I'd like to know why you're asking all these questions," he said a little querulously, picking up the bag. Then he noticed that the ball of wool had fallen out. He stooped to pick it up and push it back, tidying away the needle that was sticking out.

The men explained. They were a little apologetic but professional about their misunderstanding. After all, the facts had seemed to fit, and it was admittedly quite unusual to find a man who carried his knitting with him wherever he went.

"Oh, you should see my colleague Vladimir," Crispin said, waving the matter aside with a sweep of his hand. "He has just started on a sweater and spends all his lunch breaks at it." Not quite true, he thought, but it sounded good. After all, what difference would it have made to those guys to know that Vlad had started knitting a scarf and not a sweater?

237

At the coffee stall, the little old lady looked around carefully before taking out her mobile phone and dialling a number. The young man who ran the stall was busy with a customer, but apart from them, there was no one else around.

"All is clear, Rob," the old lady said in a low voice. "I sent the police to the car park on a wild goose chase, and I've got a few already. You can come over now, then we'll pay a little visit to the cashier as agreed."

She returned the mobile phone to her handbag and got up slowly. The young man was free now, so she put on her sweetest smile and asked him for another cup of tea, and perhaps one of those delicious scones as well? Then she settled into her chair again to wait for her accomplice to turn up.

FORTY-TWO

THREE BLIND MICE

"Here we are, dear," Mimosa said to her daughter, sitting her down on a chair in the library lobby and helping her out of her jacket. "This is where Mummy works."

She tried to sound cheerful, but she was actually feeling quite stressed. Her parents weren't able to look after Emily that morning, and there was a piece of work she absolutely had to finish. The only alternative was therefore to take the child with her for a few hours, with Simon's permission, of course.

Emily slid off the chair and began to explore her surroundings. Mummy's office looked all right, and so did the strange lady called Lucy who sat at her desk and smiled at Emily. In the office across the lobby she came upon a strange man who said he was called Simon, and he also smiled. In the office next to that one, there was one very tall man who didn't smile, and a shorter man who did. Emily liked him.

Mimosa switched her computer on and arranged their jackets on the coat hook, exchanging news with Lucy. She barely noticed Emily's disappearance until she heard her chanting in the lobby. It sounded like "Tee bine mite, tee bine mite." Mimosa smiled approvingly; good girl, she was amusing herself with a nursery rhyme she had learnt recently.

Then Emily appeared at the office door. She was waving a computer mouse to the rhythm of her chant, the wire swinging like a tail.

"Emily! Where did you get that mouse from?" Mimosa gasped. This was a bad start... why had she not put her foot down and said she couldn't complete those statistics?

"Kip," the child announced. Her mother was perplexed. What, or who, was 'kip'? She examined the computers in the lobby, but they were complete with their mice. She cast a quick glance into Simon's office in passing, but he was typing away for all he was worth. Mimosa didn't want to disturb him; there had been some more talk about the library move, and Simon was looking a little stressed. What about Vlad and Crispin's office? Mimosa put her head in and asked if they knew anything about Emily's new toy.

"Oh, I gave her mine," Crispin said stretching himself lazily. "She seemed interested in it. Clearly an intelligent child. Now I've no rodent, I won't have to do any work." He tried to lift his feet on to the desk, but the chair rolled away and Crispin nearly fell on the floor.

"Thanks, Crispin," Mimosa said. "If you can spare it... It'll keep her happy for a while, and I can get on with my work." She went back into her office, leaving Emily to march around the lobby, still chanting.

After a while, Emily had a new idea. She carefully put the mouse down on the floor and began to pull it after her by the 'tail'. This was a highly satisfying activity, and she beamed at the strange man with nice eyes who entered the library. Dr Terremoto was surprised to see a toddler there, but couldn't help being fascinated by her skilful manoeuvring of the mouse, which wasn't all that easy on the carpeted floor. Then he went into the reading room, wondering to himself whose little girl it was.

It was a quiet day, so Dr Terremoto was able to settle at his favourite workstation and start a literature search. The new Eeksperience wasn't nearly as good as My Little e-Library had been, but it still did the job of offering clinical databases, which were so much better than just an internet search if you really wanted to keep up with developments in your specialism. The librarians had been right.

The door of the reading room was pushed open. A little voice said "Pooters!" with enthusiasm. Emily trotted to the nearest computer workstation, climbed on the chair with some difficulty because the height was meant for grown-ups, and tapped at a key. Nothing happened. She thought carefully, then bent down and managed after a few attempts to press down Ctrl + Alt + Del with her nose and two fingers.

She let out a little squeak of delight when the screen lit up, but her joy was short lived – nothing else happened, however much she hammered at the keys. There was nothing except a box in the middle of the screen, and she had no idea how to get rid of the box and make the computer alive. But there was a grown-up in the room, that big man who had smiled so nicely when she was pulling her mouse along...

Mimosa finished her statistics more quickly than she had expected. It was only a one cup jobby after all, she said to herself with satisfaction and got up to put her empty coffee mug in the staff room to be washed up later by some industrious colleague. It was at that moment that she remembered her child. A wave of panic ran through her, like in those nightmares where she had forgotten about Emily's existence at the wrong moment or in the wrong place.

"Where's Emily?" she said in alarm. "Can't be anything wrong with her," was Vlad's answer as he strolled into the office. "Otherwise we would have heard a howl."

The offended mother was about to protest and say that *her* daughter never howled, but thought better of it. She instinctively started with the reading room, and there was Emily sitting on Massimo Terremoto's lap, happily watching as screen after screen was filled with the same image while the doctor executed the same commands over and over again. "Copy. Pate. Copy. Pate," she dictated.

Mimosa turned crimson with embarrassment but also with relief since the child was safe. But before she had time to thank Massimo for amusing Emily and to pick her up, there was a piercing sound that filled the room.

A fire alarm! And she was the library's fire marshal! After only a second's hesitation, she turned round and returned to the lobby to give orders to her colleagues. She knew that Emily – petrified and screaming though she was – would be all right with Massimo.

In his office, Simon stopped to listen. Strange, but the fire alarm sounded distinctly different from the usual. It was a continuous sound, but this time it consisted of two pitches, not one. He shut the door behind him and hastened into the reading room to get to the fire exit. There he discovered the reason for the unusual sound: Emily was screaming with fright at a pitch that Simon identified as a major third above the alarm sound. Marvellous child, he said to himself; she is managing to keep the pitch steady. Would his children have been capable of it at such an early age?

There were no library users around besides Dr Terremoto and two nursing students, who now filed from the lobby to the reading room with the library staff. Mimosa came last and saw her screaming daughter being carried to the fire exit in Massimo Terremoto's arms. He pushed the bar that released the door and was about to carry Emily down the steep metal steps.

"No!" Emily protested with a voice that could be heard clearly even over the fire alarm. "Em'ly walk!" She emphasised her words by arching herself back and then forward again, thereby delivering a kick to Dr Terremoto's belly that took his breath away. He put the toddler down hastily and, holding her hand, let her descend the steps herself.

The fire marshal was scandalised. There was her child and there was Dr Terremoto who should have known better, obstructing the fire escape and taking forever to make their way into the assembly area at the bottom of the steps. On the other hand, the mother in her was quite proud of Emily, who had forgotten the nasty noise and said "Vun. Two" to mark the first two steps, then turned to her escort and pointed to the next step, repeating "Vun. Two" in a demanding tone of voice.

"Three," the man said, and Emily turned back with satisfaction and negotiated the next step. Mimosa brushed past her with care, hoping the other grown-ups would do the same.

The alarm stopped abruptly as they were reaching the bottom of the fire escape. In the assembly area, an apologetic ward clerk from Slouch Ward was waiting for them. He explained that they had arranged to test their fire alarm that day but had forgotten to inform the library. Mimosa was livid, but couldn't deny that it was good practice to evacuate the library every now and then; it would do instead of organising a fire drill. She turned round to return to the library and was faced with Emily, who had just got to the bottom of the steps with a "Thirty" from Dr Terremoto. She beamed at her mother, then at the doctor and said "Again!"

***

Later on, the team assembled round the coffee pot in the staff room. It had been a little difficult to get Emily to say goodbye to Dr Terremoto. She had repeatedly, and emphatically, said "Uncle" and "Em'ly pooter *again*!" and had been at the verge of throwing a tantrum until Uncle Massimo had promised to play with her again another day. Mimosa's heart beat faster, because Massimo had looked at her and not at Emily when he said it.

Now Emily was sitting on her mother's lap holding a biscuit in each hand. She was pleased because Fiona Fatica had patted her on the head and called her library baby. Mimosa asked Emily where she had got the biscuits from. "Kip," she explained. "Liba baby," she added and fell asleep with a little sigh of satisfaction.

Simon cleared his throat to attract attention to himself. "I have an announcement to make," he said. He found it hard to keep his voice steady, but he didn't want to spoil this moment. "I had a phone call from Claire just now," he continued.

The others looked at him, puzzled. Usually a phone call from Claire Twinsett would have been reported to the team with a gloomy expression, not pleasure, which was now evident in Simon's face.

"She said the Trust has run out of money and can't move any more departments for the foreseeable future," he said triumphantly.

Lucy still looked puzzled. She wanted to know what money had to do with moving departments, so Vlad reminded her how they'd been met (and nearly knocked over, in Lucy's case) by men from St. Ain Removals that morning when the library had been relocated accidentally. There were other costs involved, refurbishment being one of them, not to mention planning the moves.

"I see," she said. "So we're safe now?"

"Yes," Simon said emphatically. Vlad and Crispin let out a tremendous cheer; Simon was impressed with their coordinating it so spontaneously. Proof of successful teamwork, he said to himself. Mimosa was indignant because they might have woken Emily, but the child simply curled up more tightly in her mother's lap. The biscuits fell from her hands to the floor, to be found there later by a disapproving Adonis.

"Good old Trust," Crispin said and stretched his legs in front of him. He cradled the coffee mug in his hands, staring into it thoughtfully for a moment. "You know what?" he said, looking up again. "We're an unusual library service, with more men than women."

"We *are* an unusual library service – full stop," Simon said, viewing his team with pride.